Aesop's Fables

伊索寓言

Original Author   Aesop
Adaptor   Scott Fisher
Illustrator   Cristian Bernardini

WORDS
450

MP3

Let's Enjoy Masterpieces!

All the beautiful fairy tales and masterpieces that you have encountered during your childhood remain as warm memories in your adulthood. This time, let's indulge in the world of masterpieces through English. You can enjoy the depth and beauty of original works, which you can't enjoy through Chinese translations.

The stories are easy for you to understand because of your familiarity with them. When you enjoy reading, your ability to understand English will also rapidly improve.

This series of *Let's Enjoy Masterpieces* is a special reading comprehension booster program, devised to improve reading comprehension for beginners whose command of English is not satisfactory, or who are elementary, middle, and high school students. With this program, you can enjoy reading masterpieces in English with fun and efficiency.

This carefully planned program is composed of 5 levels, from the beginner level of 350 words to the intermediate and advanced levels of 1,000 words. With this program's level-by-level system, you are able to read famous texts in English and to savor the true pleasure of the world's language.

The program is well conceived, composed of reader-friendly explanations of English expressions and grammar, quizzes to help the student learn vocabulary and understand the meaning of the texts, and fabulous illustrations that adorn every page. In addition, with our "Guide to Listening," not only is reading comprehension enhanced but also listening comprehension skills are highlighted.

In the audio recording of the book, texts are vividly read by professional American actors. The texts are rewritten, according to the levels of the readers by an expert editorial staff of native speakers, on the basis of standard American English with the ministry of education recommended vocabulary. Therefore, it will be of great help even for all the students that want to learn English.

Please indulge yourself in the fun of reading and listening to English through *Let's Enjoy Masterpieces*.

伊索 Aesop

    Aesop is the famous author of *Aesop's Fables*. Aesop is an English name for *Aisopos*. Supposed to have lived around 600 B.C., Aesop is known to be the slave of Iadmon of Samos and to have met a violent death in Delphi.

    Today, Aesop is known to be a storyteller for children; however, ancient Aesop's fables are not just simple children's stories. In addition, the great bulk of the fables handed down as *Aesop's Fables* are not the work of Aesop. Many of them, which were passed down through oral tradition in Greece, were adopted by Aesop and have been handed down to future generations.

    Aesop's fables don't just aim at teaching the best morals to humans. He used animals to illustrate the failings and virtues of human nature. That's why *Aesop's Fables* appeal to audiences of all ages.

Aesop's Fables are a collection of narratives that use the behavior and characteristics of animals to satirize various forms of human nature and behavior. They cleverly illustrate human nature in a simple and lucid manner.

The currently known *Aesop's Fables* are traced to a compilation of fables by a monk of the 14th century in Istanbul. However, historians are unsure how many of the tales were actually written by Aesop. More stories were added on in later years.

Some of Aesop's much-loved fables include "The Fox and the Grapes," "The Belling of the Cat," "The Goose with the Golden Eggs," "The Greedy Dog," "The Lion and the Mouse," and "The Bear and the Two Travelers."

The word fable originally refers to a fiction or myth. Therefore, fables are not just stories that teach morals, but they also provide the wisdom of life and insight into human beings.

HOW TO USE THIS BOOK
本書使用說明

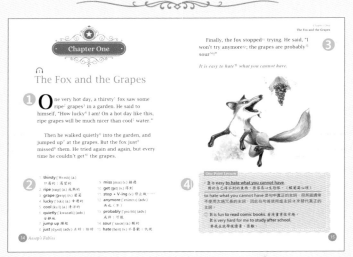

1 Original English texts

It is easy to understand the meaning of the text, because the text is rewritten according to the levels of the readers.

2 Explanation of the vocabulary

The words and expressions that include vocabulary above the elementary level are clearly defined.

B Response notes

Spaces are included in the book so you can take notes about what you don't understand or what you want to remember.

4 One point lesson

In-depth analyses of major grammar points and expressions help you to understand sentences with difficult grammar.

🎧 Audio Recording

In the audio recording, native speakers narrate the texts in standard American English. By combining the written words and the audio recording, you can listen to English with great ease.

Audio books have been popular in Britain and America for many decades. They allow the listener to experience the proper word pronunciation and sentence intonation that add important meaning and drama to spoken English. Students will benefit from listening to the recording twenty or more times.

After you are familiar with the text and recording, listen once more with your eyes closed to check your listening comprehension. Finally, after you can listen with your eyes closed and understand every word and every sentence, you are then ready to mimic the native speaker.

Then you should make a recording by reading the text yourself. Then play both recordings to compare your oral skills with those of a native speaker.

HOW TO IMPROVE
READING ABILITY
如何增進英文閱讀能力

① Catch key words

Read the key words in the sentences and practice catching the gist of the meaning of the sentence. You might question how working with a few important words could enhance your reading ability. However, it's quite effective. If you continue to use this method, you will find out that the key words and your knowledge of people and situations enables you to understand the sentence.

② Divide long sentences

Read in chunks of meaning, dividing sentences into meaningful chunks of information. In the book, chunks are arranged in sentences according to meaning. If you consider the sentences backwards or grammatically, your reading speed will be slow and you will find it difficult to listen to English.

You are ready to move to a more sophisticated level of comprehension when you find that narrowly focusing on chunks is irritating. Instead of considering the chunks, you will make it a habit to read the sentence from the beginning to the end to figure out the meaning of the whole.

❸ *Make inferences and assumptions*

Making inferences and assumptions is part of your ability. If you don't know, try to guess the meaning of the words. Although you don't know all the words in context, don't go straight to the dictionary. Developing an ability to make inferences in the context is important.

The first way to figure out the meaning of a word is from its context. If you cannot make head or tail out of the meaning of a word, look at what comes before or after it. Ask yourself what can happen in such a situation. Make your best guess as to the word's meaning. Then check the explanations of the word in the book or look up the word in a dictionary.

❹ *Read a lot and reread the same book many times*

There is no shortcut to mastering English. Only if you do a lot of reading will you make your way to the summit. Read fun and easy books with an average of less than one new word per page. Try to immerse yourself in English as often as you can.

Spend time "swimming" in English. Language learning research has shown that immersing yourself in English will help you improve your English, even though you may not be aware of what you're learning.

CONTENTS

Before You Read

crow
烏鴉

woodcutter
樵夫

oak tree
橡樹

squirrel
松鼠

The squirrel is climbing up the tree.
松鼠往樹上爬

hide
躲藏

behind
在……後面

The fox is hiding behind the bush.
狐狸躲在樹叢後面

The crow opened its mouth.
烏鴉張開嘴。

The cheese fell down.
起司掉下來。

The fox quickly got the cheese.
狐狸很快地得到起司。

clever
機智的

smart
聰明的

wise
智慧的

foolish
愚蠢的

The tree is standing with its roots in the ground.
樹木以根緊抓著地而豎立。

root
根

blossom
開花

shoot
射擊

gun
槍

chew
咀嚼

The mouse is chewing on the net.
老鼠正在咬網子。

run away
逃跑

hunter
獵人

net
網

fence
柵欄

The hunter raised his gun to shoot the fox.
獵人舉起槍要射狐狸。

get caught
被捉住

12

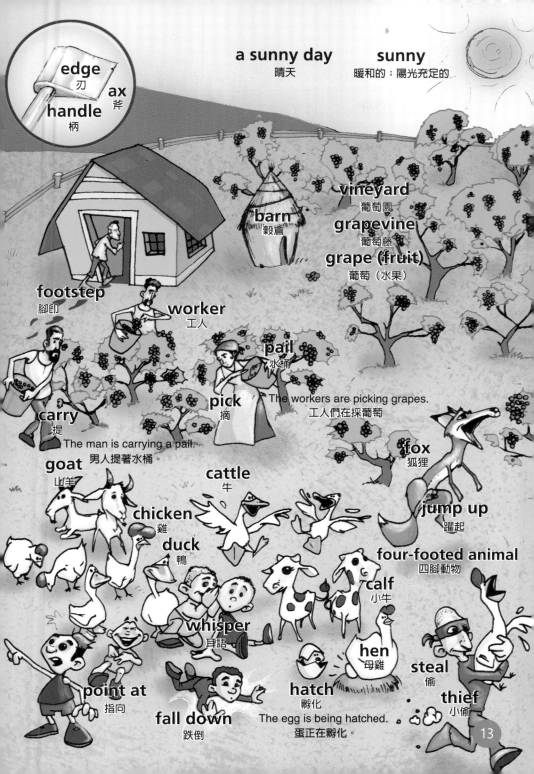

edge
刃
ax
斧
handle
柄

a sunny day
晴天

sunny
暖和的；陽光充足的

vineyard
葡萄園

barn
穀倉

grapevine
葡萄藤

grape (fruit)
葡萄（水果）

footstep
腳印

worker
工人

pail
水桶

pick
摘

The workers are picking grapes.
工人們在採葡萄

carry
提

The man is carrying a pail.
男人提著水桶。

fox
狐狸

goat
山羊

cattle
牛

jump up
躍起

chicken
雞

duck
鴨

four-footed animal
四腳動物

calf
小牛

whisper
耳語

hen
母雞

steal
偷

point at
指向

hatch
孵化

thief
小偷

fall down
跌倒

The egg is being hatched.
蛋正在孵化。

13

The Fox and the Grapes

One very hot day, a thirsty[1] fox saw some ripe[2] grapes[3] in a garden. He said to himself, "How lucky[4] I am! On a hot day like this, ripe grapes will be much nicer than cool[5] water."

Then he walked quietly[6] into the garden, and jumped up[7] at the grapes. But the fox just[8] missed[9] them. He tried again and again, but every time he couldn't get[10] the grapes.

1. **thirsty** [ˋθɜːrsti] (a.) 口渴的；渴望的
2. **ripe** [raɪp] (a.) 成熟的
3. **grape** [greɪp] (n.) 葡萄
4. **lucky** [ˋlʌki] (a.) 幸運的
5. **cool** [kuːl] (a.) 清涼的
6. **quietly** [ˋkwaɪətli] (adv.) 安靜地
7. **jump up** 躍起
8. **just** [dʒʌst] (adv.) 正好；恰好
9. **miss** [mɪs] (v.) 錯過
10. **get** [get] (v.) 得到
11. **stop + V-ing** (v.) 停止做……
12. **anymore** [ˋenimɔːr] (adv.) 再也（不）
13. **probably** [ˋprɑːbəbli] (adv.) 或許；可能
14. **sour** [ˋsauər] (a.) 酸的
15. **hate** [heɪt] (v.) 不喜歡；仇視

Finally, the fox stopped[11] trying. He said, "I won't try anymore[12]; the grapes are probably[13] sour[14]!"

It is easy to hate[15] what you cannot have.

One Point Lesson

◆ <u>**It**</u> **is easy to hate what you cannot have.**
對於自己得不到的東西，很容易心生怨恨。（酸葡萄心理）

to hate what you cannot have 是句中真正的主詞，但英語通常不使用太過冗長的主詞，因此在句首使用虛主詞 it 來替代真正的主詞。

🔵e.g. **It is fun to read comic books.** 看漫畫書很有趣。
It is very hard for me to study after school.
要我在放學後讀書，很難。

The Fox and the Crow[1]

A crow was sitting on[2] a tree branch[3] with a piece of[4] delicious cheese in its mouth. A fox saw the crow and wanted the cheese. The fox thought and thought about how it could get the cheese. Finally the fox had an idea[5].

The fox said, "What a special[6] bird! It is the most beautiful bird in the world. Are its songs as beautiful as its face?"

These kind[7] words[8] made the crow very happy, and the crow wanted to sing a song for the fox. But when the crow opened its mouth to sing, the cheese fell down[9]!

The smart[10] fox quickly[11] ran and got the cheese. Then the fox said to the crow, "You are very beautiful, but not very smart."

Don't always believe people who tell you kind things.

1. **crow** [kroʊ] (n.) 烏鴉
2. **sit on** 坐在⋯⋯ (sit-sat-sat)
3. **branch** [bræntʃ] (n.) 樹枝
4. **a piece of** 一塊；一個
5. **idea** [aɪˋdiːə] (n.) 主意；打算
6. **special** [ˋspeʃəl] (a.) 特別的
7. **kind** [kaɪnd] (a.) 友善的
8. **word** [wɜːrd] (n.) 話；文字
9. **fall down** 掉下來 (fall-fell-fallen)
10. **smart** [smɑːrt] (a.) 精明的；敏捷的
11. **quickly** [ˋkwɪkli] (adv.) 迅速地；立即

One Point Lesson

◆ Are its songs **as** beautiful **as** its face?
烏鴉的歌聲和牠的臉蛋一樣美嗎？

---

as . . . as . . . ：和⋯⋯相同（as 與 as 之間加形容詞或副詞）

e.g. My teacher is **as** old **as** my father.
我老師的年紀和我父親一樣大。

The Fox and the Woodcutter[1]

🎧 [3]

Some hunters[2] were chasing[3] a fox. The fox saw a woodcutter, and asked[4] him for help. "Please hide[5] me, kind woodcutter," the fox said. The woodcutter told the fox to go into his house.

Soon the hunters came. They asked the woodcutter, "Did you see a fox?"

The woodcutter said, "No," but pointed to his house. The hunters didn't know why the woodcutter pointed[6]. They went away[7].

After a while[8] the fox came out of[9] the house. The fox didn't say, "Thank you." The woodcutter got angry[10] at the fox. "Why don't you say thank you?" he asked.

"I wanted to thank you," the fox said. "But I saw you signal[11] to the hunters. Your words did not match[12] your actions."

You should act and speak the same—kindly.

1. **woodcutter** [ˋwʊdkʌtər] (n.) 樵夫
2. **hunter** [ˋhʌntər] (n.) 獵人
3. **chase** [tʃeɪs] (v.) 追捕
4. **ask for** 要求
5. **hide** [haɪd] (v.) 躲藏
   (hide-hid-hidden)
6. **point** [pɔɪnt] (v.) 指向；指出
7. **go away** 走開
8. **after a while** 過了一會兒
9. **out of** 從……離開
10. **get angry** 發怒
11. **signal** [ˋsɪɡnəl] (v.) 打信號
12. **match** [mætʃ] (v.) 符合；匹配

One Point Lesson

♦ **Why don't you** say thank you? 你為何不說謝謝？

Why don't you . . . ？： ❶ 你何不……？
　　　　　　　　　　　❷ 你要不要……？／你不……嗎？
　　　　　　　　　　　常使用於建議或勸說時。

e.g Why don't you come to my house this afternoon?
你何不今天下午來我家呢？

The Lion and the Mouse

🎧 4

A lion was sleeping happily[1] when a mouse ran over[2] its face. The lion woke up[3], and was very angry. The big lion caught the little mouse to kill it.

The mouse cried to the lion, "If you don't kill me, someday I will help you!"

Suddenly the lion started to laugh, "A little mouse can help a big lion like me?" The lion thought it was funny and let[4] it go.

1. **happily** [ˋhæpɪli] (adv.) 快樂地
2. **run over** 跑過 (run-ran-run)
3. **wake up** 醒來 (wake-woke-woken)
4. **let** [let] (v.) 允許；讓
5. **get caught** 被捉住
6. **net** [net] (n.) 網；陷阱
7. **roar** [rɔːr] (v.) 吼叫
8. **chew** [tʃuː] (v.) 咬
9. **hole** [houl] (n.) 洞
10. **laugh at** 嘲笑
11. **even** [ˋiːvn] (adv.) 甚至
12. **waste** [weɪst] (n.) 浪費

Soon after that day, the lion was walking in the forest. Suddenly it got caught[5] in a net[6] . The lion was very angry, and roared[7].

The mouse heard the lion and ran to help. The mouse saw the net and started chewing[8] on it. Soon the mouse chewed a big hole[9] in the net, and the lion was free!

"See," the mouse said, "you laughed at[10] me but even[11] a little mouse can help a big lion."

Being kind to someone is never a waste[12].

One Point Lesson

🔹 **Being** kind to someone is never a waste.
　幫助別人決不會徒勞無功。

---

being kind 是「親切」的意思。若是想將 eat、play 等動詞變成名詞，只要將其變成 V-ing 的形式即可，該型態稱為動名詞，與名詞一樣可當主詞或受詞。

e.g. Reading is my hobby. 閱讀是我的興趣。

The Sick Lion

One day an old, old lion realized[1] that he was too old to hunt[2] for food. The lion was sure[3] he would soon die[4]. He was very sad and went home.

As[5] he walked slowly[6] home, the lion told a bird about his sad situation[7]. Soon everyone in the forest heard about the lion's sad situation.

The other animals all felt sorry[8] for the lion. So one by one[9] they came to visit[10] the lion.

1. **realize** [ˋriːəlaɪz] (v.) 了解
2. **hunt** [hʌnt] (v.) 獵捕
3. **sure** [ʃʊr] (a.) 確信的
4. **die** [daɪ] (v.) 死亡
5. **as** [əz] (conj.) 當……時
6. **slowly** [ˋslouli] (adv.) 緩慢地
7. **situation** [͵sɪtʃuˋeɪʃn] (n.) 處境；境況
8. **feel sorry** 感到難過
9. **one by one** 一個一個地

The lion was old and weak[11], but very wise[12]. As each animal came into his home, they were easy to catch[13] and eat. Soon the old lion became happy and fat[14].

10. **visit** [ˋvɪzɪt] (v.) 拜訪
11. **weak** [wiːk] (a.) 虛弱的
12. **wise** [waɪz] (a.) 聰明的
13. **catch** [kætʃ] (v.) 捉住；捕獲
14. **fat** [fæt] (a.) 肥胖的

One Point Lesson

◆ He was **too old to** hunt for food. 他老到無法獵捕食物。

too . . . to：由於太過……導致無法……。too 是指「太過於」。

e.g. I'm **too** busy **to** play with my baby sister.
我太忙，沒有辦法和我的妹妹一起玩。

One day, early[1] in the morning, the fox came. The fox was very wise, too. He slowly came close to the lion's home. Standing outside[2], he asked if[3] the lion was feeling better[4].

"Hello, my best friend," said the lion. "Is it you? I can't see you very well. You're so far[5] away. Come closer[6], please, and tell me some kind words because I am old, and will die soon."

While[7] the lion was talking, the fox was looking closely[8] at the ground[9] in front of[10] the lion's home.

1. **early** [`ɝli] (adv.) 早地
2. **outside** [ˌaʊt`saɪd] (adv.) 在外面；在室外
3. **if** [ɪf] (conj.) 是否
4. **feel better** 覺得比較好
5. **far (away)** 遙遠的
6. **closer** [`kloʊzɚ] (a.) 更接近的（close 的比較級）
7. **while** [waɪl] (conj.) 當……的時候
8. **closely** [`kloʊsli] (adv.) 仔細地；接近地
9. **ground** [graʊnd] (n.) 地面
10. **in front of** 在……前面
11. **look up** 抬頭看
12. **nervous** [`nɝvəs] (a.) 緊張的
13. **footstep** [`fʊtstɛp] (n.) 足跡
14. **none** [nʌn] (pron.) 一個也沒有
15. **warn** [wɔrn] (v.) 警告；提醒
16. **misfortune** [mɪs`fɔrtʃuːn] (n.) 不幸

Finally the fox looked up[11], and said to the lion, "I am sorry, but I must go. I am very nervous[12] because I see the footsteps[13] of many animals going into your home, but I see none[14] coming out again!"

He is wise who is warned[15]
by the misfortunes[16] of others.

He asked **if** the lion was feeling better.
他問獅子是否覺得好些了。

if：是否……。用於間接問句。

e.g. He wants to know **if** she loves him. 他想要知道她是否愛他。
My mother asks me every day **if** I finished my homework.
我母親每天都問我功課做完了沒有。

A <The Fox and the Grapes>
True or False.

T F **1** The fox was hungry on a hot day.

T F **2** The fox saw some grapes in a garden.

T F **3** The fox jumped again and again to catch the grapes.

B <The Fox and the Crow>
Fill in the blanks with the given words.

down	close	happy	branch

1 A crow was sitting on a _____.

2 The fox walked _____ to the tree.

3 The fox's kind words made the crow very _____.

4 When the crow opened its mouth to sing, the cheese fell _____.

C <The Fox and the Woodcutter/The Lion and the Mouse>

Fill in the blanks with the given words.

when	and	but

1 The fox saw a woodcutter _____ asked him for help.

2 A lion was sleeping _____ a mouse ran over its face.

3 You laughed at me _____ even a little mouse can help a big lion.

D <The Sick Lion>

Rearrange the sentences in chronological order.

1 The old lion knew that he was too old and weak.

2 The old lion ate a lot of animals.

3 The animals visited the lion.

4 The lion told the animals about his bad situation.

_____ ⇨ _____ ⇨ _____ ⇨ _____

Help yourself!
自己來！

frightened
害怕的

lie
躺

corn
玉米

cake
蛋糕

rest
休息

finish line
終點線

tortoise/turtle
烏龜

The tortoise never stopped and kept going.
烏龜決不放棄，持續前進。

race
賽跑

judge
裁判

The fox, a judge, is standing at the finish line.
身為裁判的狐狸，站在終點線旁。

bear
熊

mouse
老鼠

crowd
一群；一堆

A crowd of animals is watching the race.
一群動物正在觀看比賽。

quietly
安靜地

The cat is coming toward
the mice quietly.
那隻貓悄悄地接近老鼠。

bell
鈴

mice
老鼠（複數）

The mice are having a picnic.
老鼠們在野餐。

Before You Read

shepherd boy
牧童

sheep
羊

dove
鴿子

starting line
起跑線

town
市區

hare/rabbit
野兔／兔子

The hare is running as fast as it could.
兔子盡力快跑。

horn
角

The lion is ready to jump on the stag.
獅子準備好要撲向雄鹿。

deer
鹿

stag
雄鹿

reed
蘆葦

thin legs
細瘦的腿

shore
岸

lake
湖

stream
溪

image/shadow
映象／倒影
The stag is looking at
its image in the lake.
雄鹿正看著
自己湖中的倒影。

calm
平靜的

clear
清澈的

quiet
安靜的

piece
塊

a piece of meat
一塊肉

The dog has a piece of meat in its mouth.
狗的嘴裡叼了一塊肉。

frog
青蛙

29

The Dog and His Shadow

A dog once had a nice piece of meat for his dinner. He was walking along with[1] the meat in his mouth, as happy as[2] a king.

On his way home[3] there was a stream[4]. The dog stopped to look into the calm[5], clear water. What did the dog see in the water?

He saw a dog looking up at him! This dog looked the same as our happy little dog, and even had a similar[6] piece of meat in its mouth!
"I'll try to get that meat, too," said the dog.

1. **walk along with** 帶著……走
2. **as . . . as** 像……一樣……
3. **on one's way home**
   在回家的路上
4. **stream** [striːm] (n.) 小溪流
5. **calm** [kɑːm] (a.) 平靜的
6. **similar** [ˋsɪmələ(r)] (a.)
   相像的；類似的
7. **as soon as** 一經……立即……
8. **bite** [baɪt] (v.) 咬住
   (bite-bit-bitten)
9. **own** [oʊn] (a.) 自己的

But as soon as[7] he tried to bite[8] the new piece of meat, his own[9] meat fell out of his mouth and into the stream! Then he saw that the other dog in the water had lost[10] his piece, too.

He went sadly[11] home. That day he only had his dreams[12] to eat.

Be careful[13] of losing something you have for something that may not exist[14].

10. **lose** [lu:s] (v.) 弄丟；失去 (lose-lost-lost)
11. **sadly** [ˋsædli] (adv.) 悲哀地
12. **dream** [dri:m] (n.) 夢；幻想
13. **careful** [ˋkɛrfəl] (a.) 小心的
14. **exist** [ɪgˋzɪst] (v.) 存在

One Point Lesson

◆ He was walking along **with** the meat in his mouth, as happy as a king. 牠嘴裡叼著肉跑來跑去，像個國王般得意洋洋。

with：在……，一邊……／在……狀態下。
本句除了描述某件事物，並說明同時間發生的情況。

e.g. Don't speak **with** your mouth full. 滿嘴食物時別開口說話。

Belling[1] the Cat

🎧 8

One day all the mice[2] came together to talk about the cat. "We must think of a plan to get away from[3] it," said one old mouse. "It has eaten too many of us. So what shall we do?"

At last[4] one proud[5] young mouse stood up. "You know, my brothers," said the young mouse, "the cat moves very quietly. We do not hear it quickly enough to[6] escape[7]. Let's tie[8] a bell around the cat's neck. Then we can hear it coming and run away.[9] "

1. **bell** [bel] (v.) 繫鈴於……
2. **mice** [maɪs] (n.) 老鼠
   （mouse 的複數）
3. **get away from** 逃脫；遠離
4. **at last** 最後；終於

5. **proud** [praʊd] (a.)
   驕傲的；自負的
6. **enough to** 足夠到可以……
7. **escape** [ɪ`skeɪp] (v.)
   逃跑；逃脫

"Yeah[10]!" shouted all the mice. "Our smart young friend has thought of an excellent[11] plan! Let's go and buy a bell."

But just then[12] an old mouse spoke. "Wait a minute," said the wise, old mouse. "Your plan is very good. But who will tie the bell on the cat?"

Then each mouse looked at another, and they all said, "Right, —who?"

It is easy to suggest[13] difficult things,
but it is hard to do them.

8. **tie** [taɪ] (v.) 繫上
9. **run away** 逃跑
10. **yeah** [jeə] (adv.)
　　（口語用法）是地
11. **excellent** [ˋɛksələnt] (a.)
　　出色的；優秀的
12. **just then** 就在那時
13. **suggest** [səˋdʒɛst] (v.) 建議

One Point Lesson

◦ We do not hear it quickly **enough** to escape.
等到聽到他的聲音再跑，我們就來不及了。

enough 前若是接形容詞或副詞，是指「足以……的程度」。

e.g. I'm old **enough** to see that movie.
我年紀夠大，可以看那部電影了。
Fast food is not good **enough** to eat every day.
速食不是那種可以天天吃的好東西。

The Hare[1] and the Tortoise[2]

🎧 9

One day a hare was making fun of[3] a tortoise for being so slow. "You think I am slow?" said the tortoise, "Let's run a race[4], and I bet[5] that I will win."

"Oh, really?" answered the hare. "Let's try and see." Soon the hare and the tortoise agreed that the fox would be the judge[6] for their race[7].

On race day both the hare and the tortoise met the fox at the starting line[8]. Both started off[9] together. Soon the hare was far[10] ahead of[11] the slow tortoise. The hare thought she could stop and take a rest[12]. She found some nice, comfortable[13] grass[14] to rest in and was soon in the deep[15] sleep.

1. **hare** [her] (n.) 野兔
2. **tortoise** [ˋtɔːrtəs] (n.) 陸龜
3. **make fun of** 取笑
4. **run a race** 賽跑
5. **bet** [bet] (v.) 打賭；斷定
6. **judge** [dʒʌdʒ] (n.) 裁判
7. **race** [reɪs] (n.) 賽跑；比賽
8. **starting line** 起跑線
9. **start off** 出發；開始
10. **far** [fɑːr] (adv.) 遠遠地
11. **ahead of** 在……之前
12. **take a rest** 休息

Meanwhile[16] the tortoise kept[17] going and going. He was slow, but he never stopped. After a nice long sleep the hare woke up. But there was a problem! She slept for too long. She jumped up and ran as fast as she could, but it was too late. The tortoise had already crossed[18] the finish line[19].

Slow and steady[20] wins the race.

13. **comfortable** [ˋkʌmfərtəbl] (a.) 舒服的
14. **grass** [græs] (n.) 草地;草坪
15. **deep** [ˋdiːp] (a.) 深深的
16. **meanwhile** [ˋmiːnwaɪl] (adv.) 其間;同時
17. **keep + V-ing** [kiːp] (v.) 持續
18. **cross** [krɔːs] (v.) 越過
19. **finish line** 終點線
20. **steady** [ˋstedɪ] (a.) 紮實穩固的

> **One Point Lesson**
>
> ◆ Let's **run a race**. 我們來賽跑吧!
> The hare thought she could stop and **take a rest**.
> 兔子想,她可以停下來休息一下。
>
> **run a race**(賽跑)/ **take a rest**(休息):
> 皆屬「特定動詞 + 特定名詞」的片語動詞。
>
> e.g. **have/take a look** 看一看　**take care** 照顧
> **take a drink** 喝

The Stag[1] at the Lake

🎧 10

One very hot day, a tall, strong stag stopped to[2] drink from a clear lake[3]. When he took a drink he could see his image[4] in the water.

"My horns[5] are so beautiful!" he said. "They are so strong and graceful[6]. But, I'm still sad because my legs are so thin[7] and ugly!"

At that moment, a lion came through[8] the forest[9], and tried to jump on the stag. The stag ran away very, very fast. The ugly legs helped[10] him run away. But the lion didn't stop following[11] the stag.

1. **stag** [stæg] (n.) 雄鹿
2. **stop to** 停下來做（其他的事）
3. **lake** [leɪk] (n.) 湖
4. **image** [ˋɪmɪdʒ] (n.) 映像
5. **horn** [hɔ:rn] (n.) 角
6. **graceful** [ˋgreɪsfl] (a.) 優美的
7. **thin** [θɪn] (a.) 細瘦的
8. **through** [θru:] (prep.) 穿過
9. **forest** [ˋfɔ:rɪst] (n.) 森林
10. **help** [help] (v.) 幫助
11. **follow** [ˋfɑ:lou] (v.) 追趕
12. **thick** [θɪk] (a.) 茂密的
13. **get caught** 被抓住
14. **pull away** 拉掉
15. **catch up with** 追上 (catch-caught-caught)
16. **kill** [kɪl] (v.) 殺死

Soon the stag ran into the forest. But the forest was very thick[12] with many trees. His beautiful horns got caught[13] in the branches! He tried to pull away[14] but he couldn't because of the long horns.

Finally the lion caught up with[15] the stag and killed[16] him.

People often forget what is really important in our lives.

One Point Lesson

His beautiful horns **got caught** in the branches!
他美麗的角被樹枝纏住！

get + 過去分詞：成為……狀態／被……

e.g. I almost **got hit** by a car. 我差點被車撞到。

The Country[1] Mouse and the City Mouse

🎧 11

One day a city mouse went to visit[2] his friend in the country.

The country mouse was very glad[3] to see his good friend.

He gave his guest[4] the best[5] dinner[6] that he could find. The country mouse was afraid[7] that there was not enough[8] food for two, so he just ate a little piece of corn[9]. His friend had some green peas[10], a piece of new cheese, and a ripe, red apple.

1. **country** [ˋkʌntri] (n.) 鄉下
2. **visit** [ˋvɪzɪt] (v.) 拜訪；探望
3. **glad** [glæd] (a.) 高興的
4. **guest** [gest] (n.) 客人
5. **best** [best] (a.) 最好的
6. **dinner** [ˋdɪnər] (n.) 晚餐
7. **afraid** [əˋfreɪd] (a.) 害怕的
8. **enough** [ɪˋnʌf] (a.) 足夠的
9. **corn** [kɔ:rn] (n.) 玉米；穀粒
10. **pea** [pi:] (n.) 豌豆

After the city mouse ate all the dinner,
he said, "How can you live in the country,
my friend? You can see nothing but[11] forest,
rivers, fields[12], and mountains. You must be[13]
very tired of[14] hearing nothing but bird songs."

11. **nothing but** 只有；只不過
12. **field** [fi:ld] (n.) 田地；農場

13. **must be** 一定是
14. **be tired of** 對……厭煩

"Come with me to the city. There you can live in a beautiful house and have good things for dinner every day. When you have lived in the city for a week, you will forget[1] all about living in the country." So the two mice went to the city.

They reached[2] the home of the city mouse at night. "You must be hungry. We walked for a long time," said the city mouse to his friend. "We will have some dinner immediately.[3]"

So they went to the dining room[4], and the city mouse found some cake and fruit.

"Help yourself[5]," he said. "There is enough for both of us."

"This is a very good dinner," said the country mouse. "You are very rich, my friend!"

Just then the door opened, and a dog came in. The mice jumped off[6] the table and ran into[7] a hole in the floor[8]. The poor[9] little country mouse was so frightened[10]!

"Do not be afraid," said his friend. "The dog cannot come in here."

1. **forget** [fərˋget] (v.) 忘記
2. **reach** [riːtʃ] (v.) 到達
3. **immediately** [ɪˋmiːdɪətli] (adv.) 立刻；直接地
4. **dining room** 餐廳
5. **help yourself** 不用客氣（自己招呼自己）
6. **jump off** 躍下
7. **run into** 跑進
8. **floor** [flɔːr] (n.) 地板
9. **poor** [pʊr] (a.) 可憐的
10. **frightened** [ˋfraɪtnd] (a.) 受驚的；害怕的

One Point Lesson

◆ **When** you have lived in the city a week, you will . . .
當你在都市住了一週後，你就會……

❶ 此時 when 不是指「……的時候」，而是「做……的話」、「……情況下」。

❷ 連接詞 when 也可以代替 if，作為假設語氣。

e.g. I'll buy you inline skates **when** you get an A in math.
如果你數學成績拿 A，我就買直排輪給你。

Then the mice went to the kitchen. They found an apple pie on the shelf [1], and were enjoying a piece of it.

At that moment[2] , they saw two bright[3] eyes watching[4] them. "The cat! The cat!" cried[5] the city mouse, and the mice quickly ran through a hole in the wall.

When the country mouse could speak, he said, "Good-bye, my friend. You can live in the city with the dogs and cats. I like my home in the country."

"In the country the birds sing to me while[6] I eat my simple[7] corn and apples. In the city the cats watch you eating your fancy[8] cake and pie. I like my corn in safety[9] better[10] than your cake in fear.[11]"

Better a simple meal[12] in peace[13]
than a fancy meal in fear.

1. **shelf** [ʃelf] (n.) 架子
2. **at that moment** 當時
3. **bright** [braɪt] (a.) 發亮的
4. **watch** [wɑːtʃ] (v.) 注視
5. **cry** [kraɪ] (v.) 叫喊
6. **while** [waɪl] (conj.) 當……時
7. **simple** [ˋsɪmpl] (a.) 簡單的
8. **fancy** [ˋfænsi] (a.) 精緻的
9. **safety** [ˋseɪfti] (n.) 安全
10. **better** [ˋbetər] (a.) 更佳的 （good 的比較級）
11. **in fear** 恐懼
12. **meal** [miːl] (n.) 一餐
13. **in peace** 和平地

One Point Lesson

◆ In the city the cats watch you eating your fancy cake and pie.
住在城市，當你吃著美味的蛋糕和派時，卻有貓在一旁虎視眈眈。

watch + 受詞 + V-ing：看著某人做……
watch（看）和感覺、聽、看等，都是透過五官來感受的動詞，稱為感官動詞。

e.g. I **heard** you **playing** the piano. 我聽到你在彈鋼琴。

A <The Dog and His Shadow>

True or False.

T F ❶ The dog got to eat a nice piece of meat.

T F ❷ The dog met another dog on the road.

T F ❸ The dog fell into the stream.

B <Belling the Cat>

Complete the sentences with antonyms of the words underlined.

❶ One mouse said one thing; another said a _____ thing.
⇨ *same*

❷ We do not hear it _____ enough to escape.
⇨ *slowly*

❸ "Wait a minute," said the _____ old mouse.
⇨ *stupid*

C <The Hare and the Tortoise /
The Stag at the Lake>

Choose the correct answer.

❶ Who was the judge for the race?

(a) The fox
(b) The dog
(c) The hare

❷ What is the opposite of the 'starting line'?

(a) Finish line
(b) End line
(c) Ending line

❸ What part of his body was the stag proud of?

(a) His tail   (b) His ears   (c) His horns

D <The Country Mouse and the City Mouse>
Fill in the blanks with the given words.

eating	fear	while

In the country the birds sing to me ❶ _____ I eat my simple corn and apples. In the city the cats watch you

❷ _____ your fancy cake and pie. I like my corn in safety better than your cake in ❸ _____."

Chapter Three

The Goose[1] With the Golden Eggs

🎧 14

T here once was a man who had a very fine[2] goose. Every day the goose laid[3] a golden egg. The man soon became[4] rich. But as he became rich, he became greedy[5].

"The goose must be gold inside[6]," he thought to himself. "I will open her, and get all the gold at once[7]."

1. **goose** [gu:s] (n.) 鵝
2. **fine** [faɪn] (a.) 美好的；上好的
3. **lay** [leɪ] (v.) 下蛋
   (lay-laid-laid)
4. **become** [bɪˋkʌm] (v.) 變成
5. **greedy** [ˋgri:di] (a.) 貪心的
6. **inside** [ˋɪnˋsaɪd] (adv.)
   在裡面；內部地

So he killed the goose, but he found no gold. The man cried and said, "I should have been happy with the golden egg each[8] day."

Sometimes greed[9] makes people do foolish[10] things.

7. **at once** 立刻
8. **each** [i:tʃ] (a.) 每個的
9. **greed** [gri:d] (n.) 貪心
10. **foolish** [ˋfu:lɪʃ] (a.) 愚蠢的;荒謬的

One Point Lesson

◦ I should have been happy with the golden egg each day. 每天有一顆金蛋,我就應該滿足了。

---

should have + 過去分詞:過去應該……
對過去沒做的事感到後悔或埋怨。

e.g. You should have told me the truth.
你應該把事實告訴我的。

I should not have eaten cookies at night.
我晚上根本就不該吃餅乾的。

The Bear and
the Travelers

🎧 15

One day, two men were traveling[1] together. They suddenly came across[2] a bear. One of the men climbed[3] quickly into a tree, and tried to hide himself among[4] its branches. The other man fell down[5] and lay[6] on the ground.

1. **travel** [ˈtrævl] (v.) 旅行
2. **come across** 偶然碰見
3. **climb** [klaɪm] (v.) 爬
4. **among** [əˈmʌŋ] (prep.) 在……之中
5. **fall down** 倒下；落下
6. **lie** [laɪ] (v.) 躺；臥 (lie-lay-lain)
7. **come up** 走過來
8. **all over** 到處；渾身
9. **hold** [hoʊld] (v.) 控制；抑制 (hold-held-held)
10. **breath** [brɛθ] (n.) 呼吸；氣息
11. **pretend to** 假裝；佯裝
12. **touch** [tʌtʃ] (v.) 接觸；碰
13. **come down** 爬下來

When the bear came up[7], and smelled him all over[8], the man held[9] his breath[10], and pretended to[11] be dead. The bear soon left him, because, as many people say, a bear will not touch[12] a dead body.

When the bear had gone, the traveler in the tree came down[13] to join[14] his friend. As a little joke[15], he asked, "What did the bear whisper[16] in your ear?"

His friend answered very seriously[17], "He told me, 'Never[18] travel with a friend who runs away when danger comes'."

A true friend is with you in good times and bad times.

14. **join** [dʒɔɪn] (v.) 相會；碰頭
15. **as a little joke** 當作一個小玩笑
16. **whisper** [`wɪspər] (v.) 低語；說悄悄話
17. **seriously** [`sɪrɪəsli] (adv.) 嚴肅地；認真地
18. **never** [`nevər] (adv.) 決不；從未

One Point Lesson

The bear soon left him, because, **as many people say**, a bear will not touch a dead body.
就像大家所說的，熊不會去碰屍體，因此那隻熊沒多久就離開了。

上句的 as many people say 作附加說明。

e.g. He is, **I think**, lying to protect her.
他呢，我想，應該是為了要保護她而說謊的吧。

The Shepherd[1] Boy and the Wolf

🎧16

There once was a young shepherd boy. He watched his sheep at the bottom[2] of a mountain. He was very lonely watching the sheep all day by himself[3].

So one day he thought of a plan to have some fun[4]. He ran down toward[5] the village, calling out[6], "Wolf! Wolf!"

1. **shepherd** [ˋʃepərd] (n.) 牧羊人
2. **bottom** [ˋbɑ:təm] (n.) 底部
3. **by himself** 他獨自一人
4. **have fun** 找樂趣
5. **toward** [tɔ:rd] (prep.) 朝；接近
6. **call out** 大喊；叫喊
7. **villager** [ˋvɪlɪdʒər] (n.) 村民
8. **for a while** 一會兒

The kind villagers[7] came out to help him, and some of them stayed with him for a while[8]. This made the boy very happy.

He decided to try the trick[9] again a few days later. Again he ran to the village shouting, "Wolf! Wolf!" Again the villagers came to help him, but they didn't see any wolves.

But shortly[10] after this, a wolf really did come out! Soon the wolf began to bother[11] the sheep. The boy again cried out, even[12] louder[13] than before, "Wolf! Wolf!"

But the villagers had been tricked twice[14] before. They thought the boy was fooling[15] them again. Because none of them went to help the boy, the wolf ate all his sheep!

No one believes a liar[16],

even when they tell the truth[17].

9. **trick** [trɪk] (n.) 惡作劇
10. **shortly** [ˋʃɔːrtli] (adv.) 不久
11. **bother** [ˋbɑːðər] (v.) 騷擾
12. **even** [ˋiːvn] (adv.) 甚至更；還
13. **louder** [ˋlaʊdər] (a.) 更大聲（loud 的比較級）
14. **twice** [twaɪs] (adv.) 兩次地
15. **fool** [fuːl] (v.) 愚弄
16. **liar** [ˋlaɪər] (n.) 騙子
17. **truth** [truːθ] (n.) 實話

The Milk-Woman and Her Pail[1]

🎧 17

A farmer's daughter was carrying[2] a pail of milk.

"I can make some money from selling[3] this milk," she thought. "That money will be enough to buy at least[4] three hundred eggs. The eggs will produce[5] about two hundred and fifty chickens. When the chickens grow, I will sell them in the market[6]. After selling the chickens, I will have enough money to buy a new dress."

1. **pail** [peɪl] (n.) 提桶
2. **carry** [ˋkæri] (v.) 挑；提
3. **sell** [sel] (v.) 賣
4. **at least** 至少
5. **produce** [prəˋduːs] (v.) 生產
6. **market** [ˋmɑːrkɪt] (n.) 市場
7. **ask** [æsk] (v.) 請求；要求

8. **marry** [ˋmæri] (v.) 結婚
9. **refuse** [rɪˋfjuːz] (v.) 拒絕
10. **hit** [hɪt] (v.) 碰撞；擊中
11. **drop** [drɑːp] (v.) 掉下；落下
12. **disappear** [ˌdɪsəˋpɪr] (v.) 消失
13. **take away** 帶走；拿走
14. **hatch** [hætʃ] (v.) 孵化

"I will wear this beautiful new dress to parties. Then all the best young men will ask[7] me to marry[8] them. But I will refuse[9] all the men and just enjoy the parties."

The young woman was enjoying her thoughts so much she didn't see a stone in the road. Suddenly her foot hit[10] the stone and she fell. She dropped[11] the pail of milk! The milk disappeared[12] into the ground, taking away[13] all of her plans.

Do not count your chickens before they are hatched[14].

After **selling** the chickens, I will have enough money to buy a new dress.
等我賣了那些雞之後，就有足夠的錢買一件新洋裝。

在使用主要子句和修飾語時，可以使用分詞構句，把修飾語的相同主詞省略，並將動詞改為現在分詞。

The Boys and the Frogs[1]

🎧18

One day, a group[2] of boys were playing by the side of a small lake. Some of the boys threw[3] stones into the water for fun[4].

A lot of frogs lived in this little lake, and they kept getting hit[5] by the stones the boys threw.

Finally, a wise old frog put his head up[6] out of the water, and said, "Boys, please don't throw stones at us."

1. **frog** [frɑːg] (n.) 青蛙
2. **group** [gruːp] (n.) 群；組
3. **throw** [θroʊ] (v.) 扔；拋
4. **for fun** 鬧著玩
5. **get hit** 被擊中
6. **put . . . up** 把……抬高
7. **only** [ˈoʊnli] (adv.) 只；僅僅
8. **hurt** [hɜːrt] (v.) 傷害
9. **cause** [kɔːz] (v.) 導致；引起
10. **pain** [peɪn] (n.) 痛苦
11. **pleasure** [ˈpleʒər] (n.) 樂趣
12. **may** [meɪ] (aux.) 可能；也許

"We are only[7] playing," said the boys.

"I know that," said the frog. "But your stones hurt[8] us! You may throw stones for fun, but your fun causes[9] us great pain[10]."

One person's pleasure[11] may[12] be another's pain.

The Miser[1]

🎧 19

A miser sold most of his land to buy a shiny[2] piece of gold. He buried[3] the gold in the ground by an old wall, and went to look at it every day.

One day, one of his workers saw the miser going to the wall and followed him. Soon the worker discovered[4] the secret[5] of the hidden[6] treasure[7]. When the miser was gone[8], he dug up[9] the gold and stole[10] it.

1. **miser** [ˋmaɪzər] (n.) 守財奴
2. **shiny** [ˋʃaɪnɪ] (a.) 閃耀的
3. **bury** [ˋberi] (v.) 埋藏；掩藏
4. **discover** [dɪˋskʌvər] (v.) 發現
5. **secret** [ˋsiːkrət] (n.) 秘密
6. **hidden** [hɪdn] (a.) 隱藏的
7. **treasure** [ˋtreʒər] (n.) 寶物
8. **be gone** 消失不見
9. **dig up** 挖掘 (dig-dug-dug)
10. **steal** [stiːl] (v.) 偷竊 (steal-stole-stolen)
11. **be stolen** 被偷

The next day the miser found that his gold had been stolen[11]. The miser cried and cried in anger[12] and sadness[13].

A neighbor[14] saw the miser crying, and found out[15] what was wrong.

He said, "Please don't cry so much. You should go and get a stone, bury it in the ground, and pretend the stone is the piece of gold. It will be just the same as[16] when the gold was there, because you never did anything[17] with the gold when you had it."

The true value[18] of money is not having it, but using it wisely[19].

12. **anger** [ˋæŋgər] (n.) 生氣
13. **sadness** [ˋsædnəs] (n.) 悲傷
14. **neighbor** [ˋneɪbər] (n.) 鄰居
15. **find out** 發現；查明
16. **the same as** 與……相同
17. **anything** [ˋenɪθɪŋ] (n.) 任何事
18. **value** [ˋvælju:] (n.) 價值
19. **wisely** [waɪzli] (adv.) 睿智地

One Point Lesson

The miser cried and cried **in anger and sadness**.
守財奴既生氣又難過，一直在那裡哭個不停。

in + 名詞：描述……的狀態

e.g. **in** peace 和平地　　　　**in** order 按照順序

A <The Goose With the Golden Eggs>
Fill in the blanks with the given words.

greedy   laid   fine   killed

❶ There once was a man who had a very _____ goose.

❷ The goose _____ a golden egg.

❸ As the man became rich, he became _____.

❹ The man _____ the goose but he found no gold.

B <The Bear and the Travelers>
True or False.

T F ❶ Two men came across a bear.

T F ❷ One man pretended to be dead.

T F ❸ The bear climbed a tree.

T F ❹ The bear killed a man.

T F ❺ One man was angry at his friend.

C <The Shepherd Boy and the Wolf /
The Boys and the Frogs>

Choose the correct answer.

❶ Which is false about the shepherd boy?

    (a) The boy was very lonely.

    (b) The boy lied to the villagers.

    (c) The wolf ate the boy.

❷ Why were the boys throwing rocks?

    (a) For fun.

    (b) To fight.

    (C) To hurt the frogs.

D <The Miser> **Cloze.**

sold	saw	buried	went

A miser **❶**_____ most of his land to buy a shiny
piece of gold. He **❷**_____ the gold in the ground by
an old wall, and **❸**_____ to look at it every day. One
of his workers **❹**_____ the miser going to the old
wall every day.

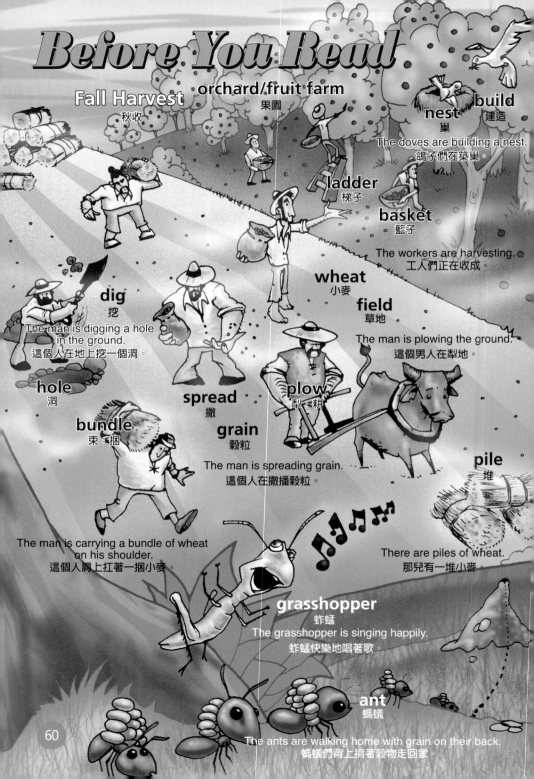

Before You Read

Fall Harvest
秋收

orchard/fruit farm
果園

nest
巢

build
建造

The doves are building a nest.
鴿子們在築巢。

ladder
梯子

basket
籃子

The workers are harvesting.
工人們正在收成。

wheat
小麥

field
草地

The man is plowing the ground.
這個男人在犁地。

dig
挖

The man is digging a hole in the ground.
這個人在地上挖一個洞。

hole
洞

spread
撒

plow
犁；耕

bundle
束；捆

grain
穀粒

The man is spreading grain.
這個人在撒播穀粒。

pile
堆

The man is carrying a bundle of wheat on his shoulder.
這個人肩上扛著一捆小麥。

There are piles of wheat.
那兒有一堆小麥。

grasshopper
蚱蜢

The grasshopper is singing happily.
蚱蜢快樂地唱著歌。

ant
螞蟻

The ants are walking home with grain on their back.
螞蟻們背上揹著穀物走回家。

60

float
浮

An ant is floating on the water.
一隻螞蟻浮在水上。

bend
彎曲

A reed is bending from the wind.
一株蘆葦隨風彎曲。

step
踩；踏

A big foot is stepping on an ant.
一隻大腳踩在螞蟻上。

bite
咬

An ant is biting the man on the foot.
一隻螞蟻咬男人的腳。

suck
吸

A frog is sucking in air.
青蛙正在吸氣。

strike
擊；打

A man is striking a tree with a bat.
男人以棒子擊打一棵樹。

bow
彎腰

A boy is bowing.
男孩在鞠躬。

explode
爆炸

The frog's big belly is exploding.
青蛙的大肚子爆炸了。

slip
滑跤

A girl is slipping on the ice.
女孩在冰上滑倒了。

take off
脫下

A boy is taking off his shirt.
男孩脫下襯衫。

ignore
不理會

A girl is ignoring a boy with flowers.
女孩不理會拿著花的男孩。

shoot
射擊

A hunter is shooting.
獵人在開槍射擊。

Chapter Four

The Ants[1] and the Grasshopper[2]

[20]

The ants and the grasshopper lived in the same big field. The ants always worked hard, and tried to prepare and harvest[3] enough food for winter.

Their happy neighbor, the grasshopper, couldn't understand them. He just ignored[4] them and kept singing.

When the first frost[5] came, it ended the work of the ants and the party of the grasshopper.

One winter day the ants were busy[6] spreading[7] their grain[8] in the sun to dry. The grasshopper was nearly dying with[9] hunger[10], so he went to the ants to ask for some food.

"Good day to you, kind neighbor," said the grasshopper, "Won't[11] you lend[12] me a little food? I will certainly[13] repay[14] you before this time next year."

1. **ant** [ænt] (n.) 螞蟻
2. **grasshopper** [ˋgræshɑːpə(r)] (n.) 蚱蜢
3. **harvest** [ˋhɑːrvɪst] (v.) 收穫
4. **ignore** [ɪˋgnɔː(r)] (v.) 不理會
5. **frost** [frɔːst] (n.) 霜
6. **be busy + V-ing** 忙於……
7. **spread** [spred] (v.) 散布；攤開
8. **grain** [greɪn] (n.) 穀粒；穀物
9. **die with** 因……而死亡
10. **hunger** [ˋhʌŋgə(r)] (n.) 飢餓
11. **won't** 為 will not 的縮寫
12. **lend** [lend] (v.) 借出
13. **certainly** [ˋsɜːrtnli] (adv.) 無疑地；必定
14. **repay** [rɪˋpeɪ] (v.) 償還；報答

"Why don't you have any food of your own[1]?" asked an old ant. "There was a lot of food in the big field all summer[2]. What did you do?"

"Oh," said the grasshopper, forgetting[3] his hunger, "I sang all day long, and all night long."

"Well, then," said the ant. "If you can sing all summer, you should dance all winter[4]."

And the old ant went back[5] to her work singing the ant song. "We ants never borrow[6]; we ants never lend."

Don't forget to prepare for bad times, even[7] during[8] good times.

1. **own** [oun] (a.) 自己的
2. **all summer** 整個夏天
3. **forget** [fər`gɛt] (v.) 忘記
4. **all winter** 整個冬天
5. **go back** 回去
6. **borrow** [`bɑːroʊ] (v.) 借入
7. **even** [`iːvn] (adv.) 甚至；即使
8. **during** [`dʊrɪŋ] (prep.) 在某期間

One Point Lesson

◈ I sang **all day long**, and **all night long**.
我不分晝夜，唱了一整天的歌。

---

all day long：一整天　　**all night long**：一整夜
long 放在名詞後面，不僅可代表時間，也可代表長度或距離。

e.g. Our vacation was one month **long**.
我們的假期長達一個月。

The Ant
and the Dove[1]

[22] An ant was walking by the river one day, and said to himself, "How nice and cool this water looks! I must drink some of it."

As he began to drink, his foot slipped[2], and he fell in[3].

"Oh, somebody, please, help me, or I will die!" cried the ant.

A dove sitting in a tree over the river heard him, and threw[4] him a leaf. "Climb upon[5] the leaf," said the dove, "and you will float[6] to the riverside."

The ant climbed upon the leaf, and the wind blew[7] it to the shore[8], and he stepped[9] upon dry land again.

"Thank you, kind dove," said the ant as he went home. "You have saved[10] my life, and I wish I could[11] do something for you."

"Good-bye," said the dove. "Be careful not to fall in again."

1. **dove** [dʌv] (n.) 鴿子
2. **slip** [slɪp] (v.) 滑落；失足
   (slip-slipped-slipped)
3. **fall in** 掉進去
4. **throw** [θroʊ] (v.) 投；擲
5. **climb upon** 爬到……上
6. **float** [floʊt] (v.) 漂浮

7. **blow** [bloʊ] (v.) 吹；刮
   (blow-blew-blown)
8. **shore** [ʃɔ:(r)] (n.) 河岸
9. **step** [step] (v.) 舉步；踏到
10. **save** [seɪv] (v.) 救
11. **I wish I could** 我希望我可以
    ……（代表現在不行）

One Point Lesson

◆ **How nice and cool this water looks!**
這水看起來很棒很涼耶！

How + 形容詞／副詞（ + 主詞 + 動詞）！：感嘆的句型。
how 是「多麼地、實在是」的意思，是強調用語。

e.g. **How** nice! 真好！
How kind he is! 他人真的很好！

A few days later, when the dove was busy building[1] her nest[2], the ant saw a hunter raising[3] his gun[4] to shoot[5] her.

The ant ran quickly, and bit[6] the man's foot very hard. He cried, "Oh! Oh!" and dropped his gun. This surprised[7] the dove, and she flew away[8].

1. **build** [bɪld] (v.) 建造
2. **nest** [nest] (n.) 巢；窩
3. **raise** [reɪz] (v.) 舉起
4. **gun** [gʌn] (n.) 槍
5. **shoot** [ʃuːt] (v.) 開（槍）
   (shoot-shot-shot)
6. **bite** [`baɪt] (v.) 咬 (bite-bit-bit)
7. **surprise** [sərˋpraɪz] (v.) 驚嚇

After the hunter was gone, the dove came back[9] to her nest. "Thank you, my little friend," she said. "You have saved my life."

The little ant jumped for joy[10], because he had been able to[11] help the kind dove.

One kind act brings[12] another.

8. **fly away** 飛走
9. **come back** 回來
10. **for joy** 欣喜地
11. **be able to** 能夠
12. **bring** [brɪŋ] (v.) 帶來

The Frog and the Ox

O ne day an ox was walking in a wet[1] field. He accidentally[2] put[3] his foot on a family of young frogs and killed most of them. However, one escaped and ran off[4] quickly to his mother.

"Oh, Mother!" he said. "While we were playing, a really big four-footed animal[5] stepped on us."

"Big?" asked the old frog. "How big?" She sucked in air to make herself larger and said, "As big as this?"

"Oh!" said the little frog. "Much, much bigger than that."

"Well, was it this big?" She sucked in even more air.

"Oh, mother, it was much bigger than that. So please stop sucking in[6] air, you might[7] hurt yourself."

The mother frog didn't like her little one to doubt[8] her abilities[9], so she tried again to become bigger. But this time she tried so hard that her body exploded[10].

Over-confidence[11] in your abilities can lead to[12] personal[13] destruction[14].

1. **wet** [wet] (a.) 潮濕的
2. **accidentally** [ˌæksɪˋdentəli] (adv.) 意外地
3. **put . . . on** 把……放在……上
4. **run off** 逃走
5. **four-footed animal** 四足動物
6. **suck in** 吸進
7. **might** [maɪt] (aux.) 可能
8. **doubt** [daʊt] (v.) 懷疑；不相信
9. **ability** [əˋbɪləti] (n.) 能力
10. **explode** [ɪkˋsploʊd] (v.) 爆炸
11. **over-confidence** 過度自信
12. **lead to** 導致
13. **personal** [ˋpɜːrsənl] (a.) 個人的
14. **destruction** [dɪˋstrʌkʃən] (n.) 毀滅；破壞

A <The Ants and the Grasshopper>
True or False.

☐T ☐F **❶** The ants helped the grasshopper in the winter.

☐T ☐F **❷** The grasshopper played with the ants in the winter.

☐T ☐F **❸** The ants prepared for winter.

B Choose the correct answer.

❶ The grasshopper _____ more than the ants.

(a) worked

(b) prepared

(c) played

❷ The ants _____ more than the grasshopper.

(a) worked

(b) played

(c) sang

C <The Ant and the Dove>

Fill in the blanks with the given words.

after	or	and	when

❶ Somebody please help me, _____ I will die!

❷ A dove heard him _____ threw him a leaf.

❸ _____ the dove was busy building her nest, the ant saw a hunter.

❹ _____ the hunter was gone, the dove came back to her nest.

D <The Frog and the Ox>

Rearrange the following sentences in chronological order.

❶ The body of the mother frog exploded.

❷ One frog escaped and ran off to tell his mother.

❸ The mother frog sucked in air.

❹ The ox put his foot on the frogs and killed most of them.

_____ ⇨ _____ ⇨ _____ ⇨ _____

Chapter Five

The Wind and the Sun

Long, long ago, the wind and the sun were talking to each other. They could not decide who was stronger than the other. To answer the question, they agreed to try something.

Watching a passing[1] traveler, they decided to see which of them could take off[2] the man's coat first.

The wind began to blow a cold and powerful wind. But the stronger the wind blew, the tighter[3] the man held[4] on to his coat.

---

1. **pass** [pæs] (v.) 經過;路過
2. **take off** 脫下
3. **tight** [taɪt] (a.) 緊的
4. **hold** [hould] (v.) 緊抓;握住
   (hold-held-held)
5. **turn** [tɜːrn] (n.) 輪流時各自的
   一次機會
6. **behind** [bɪˋhaɪnd] (prep.)
   在……後面
7. **shine** [ʃaɪn] (v.) 照耀

Next, it was the sun's turn[5]. Coming out from behind[6] the clouds, the sun shone[7] its warm, comfortable light down on the traveler.

The traveler felt the gentle[8] warmth[9] on his shoulders. Finally, he sat down and took off his coat. It was clear[10] that the sun had won.

Kindness[11] can be stronger than harshness[12].

8. **gentle** [ˋdʒentl] (a.) 溫和的
9. **warmth** [wɔːrmθ] (n.) 溫暖
10. **clear** [klɪr] (a.) 明顯清楚的

11. **kindness** [ˋkaɪndnəs] (n.) 仁慈
12. **harshness** [ˋhɑːrʃnəs] (n.) 嚴厲

> **One Point Lesson**
>
> ◆ **The stronger** the wind blew, **the tighter** the man held on to his coat. 風吹得越強,男人越是緊緊地抓住外套。
>
> ---
>
> **the 比較級(+主詞+動詞), the + 比較級(+主詞+動詞):**
> 越是……,就越……
>
> **e.g.** **The more** you know, **the more** interesting it is.
> 你了解得越多,就會越覺得有趣。

75

The Oak[1] and the Reed[2]

🎧 26

On the side of a river grew a tall oak tree. It stood[3] with its roots[4] firmly[5] in the ground, and its head high in the air, and said to itself, "How strong I am! Nothing can make me bow[6]. I am taller and stronger than all the other trees."

But one day there was a storm[7]. The strong wind came and struck[8] the proud[9] oak. The tree fell into[10] the river. As the water carried it away[11], it passed by[12] a thin reed that grew on the riverside.

1. **oak** [oʊk] (n.) 橡樹
2. **reed** [ri:d] (n.) 蘆葦
3. **stand** [stænd] (v.) 站立；豎立
4. **root** [ru:t] (n.) 根
5. **firmly** [ˋfɜ:rmli] (adv.) 堅固地
6. **bow** [baʊ] (v.) 彎腰；屈身
7. **storm** [stɔ:rm] (n.) 暴風雨
8. **strike** [ˋstraɪk] (v.) 襲擊 (strike-struck-struck)
9. **proud** [praʊd] (a.) 驕傲的
10. **fall into** 掉進去
11. **carry away** 帶走

The little reed stood up tall, and looked at the poor broken[13] tree. "Hello, reed," said the tree, "Why didn't you break[14] when the wind came? You are so little and weak."

"Oh, poor tree," said the reed, "I bent[15] and moved until the wind had passed. It must go where it is sent, but it will not hurt those who are not proud."

Sometimes you have to bend low to succeed[16].

12. **pass by** 經過
13. **broken** [`broʊkən] (a.) 損壞的
14. **break** [`breɪk] (v.) 折斷
    (break-broke-broken)
15. **bend** [bend] (v.) 彎曲
    (bend-bent-bent)
16. **succeed** [sək`siːd] (v.) 成功

> **One Point Lesson**
>
> On the side of a river grew a tall oak tree.
> 河邊長著一棵高大的橡樹。
>
> 要強調副詞子句的內容，可將句中主詞與動詞位置調換，改成倒裝句。
>
> e.g. Down **came the shower**. 陣雨淅瀝嘩啦地落下。

77

The Ax[1] and the Trees

🎧 27

Once upon a time[2], a man went to a forest.
He asked the trees if[3] they would give him
some wood to make a handle[4] for his ax.
The trees thought this was very little[5] to ask,
and they gave him a good piece of hard wood.

But as soon as the man fit[6] the handle to his ax,
he started to cut down[7] all the best trees in the
forest.

As they crashed[8] painfully[9] to the ground, the trees said sadly to each other, "We suffer[10] because of our foolishness[11]."

Only a fool[12] would give their enemy[13] the tools[14] to destroy[15] them.

1. **ax** [æks] (n.) 斧
2. **once upon a time** 從前
3. **ask . . . if** 請求……是否可以
4. **handle** [ˋhændl] (n.) 柄；把手
5. **little** [ˋlɪtl] (a.) 微不足道的
6. **fit** [fɪt] (v.) 安裝
7. **cut down** 砍下
8. **crash** [kræʃ] (v.)
   （發出猛烈撞擊聲地）倒下

9. **painfully** [ˋpeɪnfəli] (adv.)
   痛苦地
10. **suffer** [ˋsʌfə(r)] (v.) 受苦
11. **foolishness** [ˋfuːlɪʃnəs] (n.) 愚蠢
12. **fool** [fuːl] (n.) 傻瓜；蠢人
13. **enemy** [ˋenəmi] (n.) 敵人
14. **tool** [tuːl] (n.) 工具
15. **destroy** [dɪˋstrɔɪ] (v.) 毀壞；消滅

The Rose and the Amaranth[1]

🎧 28

A rose and an amaranth blossomed[2] side by side[3] in a garden. One nice summer day, the amaranth said to its neighbor, "I envy[4] your beauty and your sweet smell[5] ! Now I understand why everyone loves you."

1. **amaranth** [ˈæməˌrænθ] (n.) 【詩】不凋花;【植】莧菜
2. **blossom** [ˈblɑːsəm] (v.) 開花
3. **side by side** 相鄰;一起
4. **envy** [ˈenvi] (v.) 嫉妒;羨慕
5. **smell** [smel] (n.) 香味;氣味
6. **bloom** [bluːm] (v.) 開花
7. **petal** [ˈpetl] (n.) 花瓣
8. **wither** [ˈwɪðə(r)] (v.) 枯萎;凋謝
9. **fall** [fɔːl] (v.) 落下;掉落
10. **fade** [feɪd] (v.) 凋謝;褪色

But the rose replied sadly, "Ah, my friend, I bloom[6] only for a short time. Soon my petals[7] will wither[8] and fall[9] , and then I will die. But your flowers never fade[10], even if[11] they are cut. They last[12] forever[13] ."

"Greatness[14] brings its own problems."

11. **even if** 即使
12. **last** [læst] (v.) 持續；維持
13. **forever** [fər`evə(r)] (adv.) 永遠地
14. **greatness** [`greɪtnəss] (n.) 偉大；高尚

One Point Lesson

But your flowers never fade, **even if** they are cut.
但即使你被剪下來，花瓣也絕不會凋落。

even if：即使……。連接兩個子句的連接詞。

e.g. I was happy, **even if** she didn't like me.
即使她不喜歡我，我還是很快樂。

The Boy and the Nuts[1]

A little boy once put his hand into a jar[2]. The jar was full of[3] nuts. He tried to take out[4] as many as[5] his hand could hold. But when he tried to pull[6] his hand out, it was too large for the narrow neck[7] of the jar.

1. **nut** [nʌt] (n.) 堅果；核果
2. **jar** [dʒɑ:(r)] (n.)
   （無把手之）廣口瓶
3. **be full of** 充滿
4. **take out** 拿出來
5. **as many as** 和……一樣多
6. **pull out** 拿出

7. **neck** [nek] (n.)
   （瓶、壺等的）頸
8. **lose** [lu:s] (v.) 失去
9. **be happy with** 滿意於……
10. **half** [hæf] (n.) 一半
11. **at once** 立刻；馬上

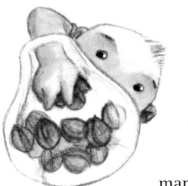

The boy didn't want to lose[8] his nuts. The little boy started to cry. An adult saw the little boy standing close by, and told him something wise.

"Be happy with[9] half[10] as many, and you will get them easily."

Do not try too much at once[11].

◊ Be happy with **half as many**, and you will get them easily.
只拿一半，你就覺得心滿意足的話，那你很輕易就能拿得到了。

as many 後面省略了 **as you hold**
as . . . as 前可加 **half**（……的一半）、**two times**（……的兩倍）或 **three times**（……的三倍）。

e.g. The U.S. is **fifty times as large as** my country.
美國是我們國家大小的 50 倍。

A \<The Wind and the Sun>

Complete the sentences with antonyms of the words underlined.

❶ The wind began to blow coldly and _____.

⇔ weakly

❷ The stronger the wind blew, the _____ the man held on to his coat. ⇔ looser

❸ Finally, he sat down and _____ his coat.

⇔ put on

❹ It was clear that the sun had _____.

⇔ lost

B \<The Oak and the Reed>

True or False.

T F ❶ The reed lived because it was stronger.

T F ❷ The oak thought he was strong.

T F ❸ The reed was broken by the wind.

Appendixes

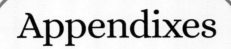

1 Basic Grammar

要增強英文閱讀理解能力，應練習找出英文的主結構。
要擁有良好的英語閱讀能力，首先要理解英文的段落結構。

「英文的主要句型結構比較簡單」

所有的英語文章都是由主詞和動詞所構成的，無論文章再怎麼長或複雜，它的架構一定是「主詞和動詞」，而「補語」和「受詞」是做補充主詞和動詞的角色。

主詞 — 動詞

某樣東西　　如何做
（人、事、物）

He **runs** (very fast).
他　　跑　　（非常快）

It **is raining** .
雨　　正在下

主詞 — 動詞 — 補語　（補充的話）

某樣東西　　如何做　　怎麼樣
（人、事、物）

This **is** **a cat** .
這　　是　　一隻貓。

The cat **is** very **big** .
那隻貓　　是　非常　大

主詞 〜 動詞 〜 受詞

某樣東西 (人、事、物)	如何做	什麼

> 人，事物，兩者皆是受詞

I like you .

我 喜歡 你。

You gave me some flowers .

你 給 我 一些花

主詞 〜 動詞 〜 受詞 〜 補語

某樣東西 (人、事、物)	如何做	什麼	怎麼樣／什麼

You make me happy .

你 使（讓） 我 幸福（快樂）

I saw him running .

我 看到 他 跑

　　其他修飾語或副詞等，都可以視為為了完成句子而臨時、額外、特別附加的，閱讀起來便可更加輕鬆；先具備這些基本概念，再閱讀《伊索寓言》的部分精選篇章，最後做了解文章整體架構的練習。

<The Fox and the Grapes>

One very hot day, **a thirsty fox** saw some **ripe grapes** in a garden.

一個炎熱的日子 一隻口渴的狐狸 看到 一些 成熟的葡萄 在花園裡

He said to himself, "How lucky **I** am !"

他 說 對他自己 多麼 幸運 我 是

On a hot day like this **ripe grapes** will be much nicer than cool water."

像這樣炎熱的日子 成熟的葡萄 會 遠 更好 比冷水

Then he walked quietly into the garden, and
於是 他 走 靜靜地 進花園 並

jumped up at the grapes.
往上跳 朝葡萄

But the fox just missed them .
但 狐狸 正好 錯過 它們

Then he tried again and again, but
於是 他 試 一次又一次 但

every time he couldn't get the grapes .
每一次 他 摶不到 葡萄

Finally, the fox stopped trying after a long time
終於 狐狸 停止 嘗試 長時間後

He said , " I won't try anymore; the grapes are
他 說 我 不試 再也 葡萄 是

probably sour !"
可能 酸的

\<The Sick Lion\>

An old, old lion realized one day
一隻很老很老的獅子 發現 有一天

that he was too old to hunt for food .
他太老無法獵捕食物

The lion was sure he would soon die.
獅子 是 確定的 他很快會死

The lion was very sad and went home.
獅子 是 非常 傷心 並 回去 家裡

As he walked slowly home,
當 他 走 慢慢地 家

the lion told a bird about his sad situation.
獅子　告訴　一隻鳥　　關於他的情況

Soon everyone in the forest heard about the lion's sad situation.
很快　每個人　　森林裡　　聽到　　　關於獅子悲慘的情況

The other animals all felt sorry for the lion.
其他動物　　全部 感到　難過　為獅子

One by one the animals came to visit the lion.
一個接一個　　動物　　來　　拜訪獅子

The lion was old and weak , but very wise .
獅子　是　　老和衰弱　　但　非常聰明

As each animal came into his home to visit,
當　每個動物　來　　進去他家　　拜訪

they were easy to catch and eat.
他們　是　容易　抓住和吃

Soon the old lion became happy and fat .
很快　老獅子　變得　快樂與肥胖

One day, early in the morning, the fox came .
一天　　　一大早　　狐狸　來

Everybody knew the fox was very wise too .
每個人　知道　狐狸也很聰明

The fox slowly came close to the lion's home.
狐狸　慢慢地　來到　接近獅子家

Standing outside he asked if the lion was feeling better .
站在屋外　他　問　獅子是否覺得好一點

"Hello, my best friend," said the lion , "is it you?"
嗨　我的好朋友　說　獅子　是你嗎

Guide to Listening Comprehension

When listening to the story, use some of the techniques shown below. If you take time to study some phonetic characteristics of English, listening will be easier.

Get in the flow of English.

English creates a rhythm formed by combinations of strong and weak stress intonations. Each word has its particular stress that combines with other words to form the overall pattern of stress or rhythm in a particular sentence.

When you are speaking and listening to English, it is essential to get in the flow of the rhythm of English. It takes a lot of practice to get used to such a rhythm. So, you need to start by identifying the stressed syllable in a word.

Listen for the strongly stressed words and phrases.

In English, key words and phrases that are essential to the meaning of a sentence are stressed louder. Therefore, pay attention to the words stressed with a higher pitch. When listening to an English recording for the first time, what matters most is to listen for a general understanding of what you hear. Do not try to hear every single word. Most of the unstressed words are articles or auxiliary verbs, which don't play an important role in the general context. At this level, you can ignore them.

Pay attention to liaisons.

In reading English, words are written with a space between them. There isn't such an obvious guide when it comes to listening to English. In oral English, there are many cases when the sounds of words are linked with adjacent words.

For instance, let's think about the phrase "take off," which can be used in "take off your clothes." "Take off your clothes" doesn't sound like [teɪk ɔːf] with each of the words completely and clearly separated from the others. Instead, it sounds as if almost all the words in context are slurred together, [ˈteɪkɔːf], for a more natural sound.

Shadow the voice of the native speaker.

Finally, you need to mimic the voice of the native speaker. Once you are sure you know how to pronounce all the words in a sentence, try to repeat them like an echo. Listen to the book again, but this time you should try a fun exercise while listening to the English.

This exercise is called "shadowing." The word "shadow" means a dark shade that is formed on a surface. When used as a verb, the word refers to the action of following someone or something like a shadow. In this exercise, pretend you are a parrot and try to shadow the voice of the native speaker.

Try to mimic the reader's voice by speaking at the same speed, with the same strong and weak stresses on words, and pausing or stopping at the same points.

Experts have already proven this technique to be effective. If you practice this shadowing exercise, your English speaking and listening skills will improve by leaps and bounds. While shadowing the native speaker, don't forget to pay attention to the meaning of each phrase and sentence.

Step 1 Listen to what you want to shadow many times. Start out by just trying to shadow a few words or a sentence.

 Step 2 Mimic the CD out loud. You can shadow everything the speaker says as if you are singing a round, or you also can speak simultaneously with the recorded voice of the native speaker.

 Step 3 As you practice more, try to shadow more. For instance, shadow a whole sentence or paragraph instead of just a few words.

3 Listening Guide

以下為《伊索寓言》各章節的前半部。一開始若能聽清楚發音，之後就沒有聽力的負擔。先聽過摘錄的章節，之後再反覆聆聽括弧內單字的發音，並仔細閱讀各種發音的說明。以下都是以英語的典型發音為基礎，所做的簡易說明，即使這裡未提到的發音，也可以配合音檔反覆聆聽，如此一來聽力必能更上層樓。

Chapter One page 14 🎧 30

One very hot day a thirsty (**1**) saw some ripe grapes in a garden. He (**2**) (   ) himself, "How lucky I am! On a hot day like this ripe grapes will be much nicer than cool (**3**)."

1 **fox:** 母音發 [ɑ:] 的音，發 f 音時以上排牙齒稍微咬住下唇發音，不要和 p 的音混淆。

2 **said to:** said 的 d 和緊接在後的 to 合在一起發音。當相鄰的兩個發音相同或相近時，會合起來發一個音。

3 **water:** t 夾在兩個母音中間時，會發 [d] 的音，這是具代表性的美式發音。

> A dog once had a nice (**❶**) ( ) meat for his dinner. He was walking along with the meat in his mouth, as happy (**❷**) ( ) king. On his way home there was a stream. The dog (**❸**) ( ) look into the calm, clear water.

❶ piece of: piece 的 -ce 與 of 連在一起發音，聽起來像一個單字；of 前面的單字若是以子音結束，大部分會變成連音，而 -f（發 [v] 的音）的音也幾乎聽不到。

❷ as a: 也屬於連音。「as a + 名詞」是常使用的句型，as 和 a 大致上和前面所敘述的相同，都是連著發音。

❸ stopped to: stopped 的 -ed（發 [t] 的音）和 to 連起來發一個音。有時很難區分是現在式的 stop to ，還是過去式的 stopped to。在此情況下，只能依照前後文的字句來判斷。此外，也有與 stopped 一樣，s 後若緊接著 [t]、[p]、[k] 的音，常會由無聲轉變為有聲的發音。

There once (❶) ( ) man who had a very (❷) goose. Every day the goose laid a golden egg. The man soon (❸) rich. But as he became rich, he became greedy. "The goose (❹) ( ) gold inside," he thought to himself.

❶ **was a:** was 的 -s 與 a 變成連著發音，因此聽起來像一個單字。a 若非在句中具重要性的意義，會與前一個單字連著發音，發出的音聽起來很弱。

❷ **fine:** [f] 若不小心地發音，聽者可能會將 fine 聽成 pine，因此要正確地區分 [f] 和 [p] 的發音。

❸ **became:** 重音在第二音節。相對的第一音節發音較弱，唸快一點的話，聽起來可能會像 came。

❹ **must be:** 兩個單字連起來發音。在這裡 must 的 [t] 音不唸出來。美式英語中，當三個子音連續出現時，中間的音會被省略。

The ants and the grasshopper (❶) ( ) the same big field. The ants always worked hard and tried to (❷) and (❸) enough food for winter. Their happy neighbor, the grasshopper, couldn't understand them. He just ignore them and kept singing.

❶ **lived in:** lived 的 -ed 與 in 像一個單字般連在一起發音。現在式 live in，會發出像 living 的連音。因屬於時常出現的發音型態，讀者應熟記此類發音法。

❷ **prepare:** 快速發出 pre- 或 pro- 等音時，聽起來像是 per 或 por 的音，這樣的唸法是為了更方便發音。

❸ **harvest:** 重音在第一音節，最後的 -st 發輕音即可。

Chapter Five page 74 🎧34

Long, long ago, the (❶) ( ) the sun were talking to each other. They (❷) not decide who was stronger than the other. To answer the question, they agreed to try something. Watching a passing traveler, they decided to see which of them could (❸) ( ) the man's coat first.

❶ **wind and:** wind 與 and 連著發音。因為 and 通常無重要或完整的意義，所以在句中幾乎無法聽到 and 的音，最後的 [d] 音幾乎消失，聽起來會類似 [n] 或 [en] 的音。

❷ **could:** could 和 and 的情況相同，屬於不具有重要意義的單字，其發音非常微弱，快速略過而已。

❸ **take off:** take 與 off 為連音，聽起來像只有一個單字。片語的意義固然重要，但也應熟記此類發音法。

Listening Comprehension

🎧 35 **A** Listen to the CD and fill in the blanks.

❶ The mother frog _____ from sucking in too much air.

❷ A _____ lives in a farm-house.

❸ On our next vacation we're going to _____ to the beach.

❹ Some people live in the city; other people live comfortably in the _____.

❺ The mice wanted to put a _____ on the cat so they could hear it.

❻ A _____ is small and likes cheese.

❼ The _____ was deep, clear and had a lot of fish.

🎧 36 **B** Listen to the CD. Write down the sentences and choose True or False.

Ⓣ Ⓕ ❶ ....

Ⓣ Ⓕ ❷ ....

Ⓣ Ⓕ ❸ ....

Ⓣ Ⓕ ❹ ....

C Listen to the CD and choose the correct answer.

1 _____?

    (a) Work hard.

    (b) Play hard.

    (c) Borrow from friends.

2 _____?

    (a) Give up if something is difficult.

    (b) Try hard even if something is difficult.

    (c) Complain if something is difficult.

3 _____?

    (a) People will help liars.

    (b) It's OK to lie if you're lonely.

    (c) Never lie.

4 _____?

    (a) A person who loves food.

    (b) A person who loves sleeping.

    (c) A person who loves money.

5 _____?

    (a) A person who takes care of wolves.

    (b) A person who takes care of sheep.

    (c) A person who takes care of fields.

Translation

　　伊索是著作《伊索寓言》（*Aesop's Fables*）的名作家。伊索是拉丁文 *Aisopos* 的英文名，據說他生於西元前 600 年左右。伊索曾在（希臘）薩摩斯島（Samos）上為雅德蒙（Iadmon）的奴隸，後於德爾菲（Delphi）一地遇害慘死。

　　現今，伊索以作為孩子們的說書人聞名，然而伊索的寓言不只是簡單的兒童故事。此外，大量以《伊索寓言》之名流傳的寓言故事，並非出自伊索之筆。許多故事因希臘口傳傳統流傳下來，經伊索改編後再傳承後世。

　　伊索的寓言故事並非僅旨在教導人類道德精神，他也以動物形象，闡明出人性的敗壞與良善。這也是各年齡層的讀者深受《伊索寓言》吸引的原因。

Aesopus moralisatus, 1485

故事簡介

《伊索寓言》是以動物的行為個性，諷刺各種人性本質和舉止的故事文集。這些故事以簡明清晰的筆法，巧妙體現了人性特質。

現今所知的《伊索寓言》，可追溯至 14 世紀伊斯坦堡一名修道士的寓言合輯。然而，因許多故事都是晚期加入的，歷史學家不確定有多少故事真正出自伊索。

伊索一些深受喜愛的寓言故事有：〈狐狸與葡萄〉（*The Foxes and the Grapes*）、〈給貓掛鈴鐺〉（*The Belling of the Cat*）、〈下金蛋的鵝〉（*The Goose with the Golden Eggs*）、〈狗和影子〉（*The Greedy Dog*）、〈獅子與老鼠〉（*The Lion and the Mouse*）和〈熊與旅人〉（*The Bear and the Two Travelers*）。

寓言故事（fable）原指虛構作品（fiction）或神話（myth）。因此，寓言故事不只教導道德倫理，同時也傳授了人生智慧與人性洞見。

[第 一 章] 狐狸與葡萄

`p. 14–15` 一個大熱天，一隻口渴的狐狸見到果園裡的葡萄，自言自語道：「運氣真好啊！天氣這麼熱，成熟的葡萄比清涼的水更能消暑呢。」

於是他靜悄悄地走進果園，往上跳要摘葡萄，但就是怎麼也搆不著，他試了一次又一次，每一次都摘不到葡萄。

最後，狐狸放棄了，他說：「我再也不跳了，葡萄搞不好是酸的呢。」

對於自己得不到的東西，很容易心生怨恨（吃不到葡萄說葡萄酸）。

狐狸與烏鴉

`p. 16–17` 一隻烏鴉停在一根樹枝上，嘴裡啣著一塊美味的起司。狐狸看到了，也想要烏鴉嘴裡的那塊起司。他心忖，該怎麼弄到那塊起司呢？最後，他想到了一個法子。

狐狸說：「好特別的鳥啊！這真是世界上最美麗的鳥了，只是不知道他的歌聲是不是和外表一樣美呢？」

這些讚美的話，讓烏鴉聽得心花怒放，便想為狐狸一展歌喉。然而，就在他張口高歌時，起司掉了下來！

精明的狐狸便迅速跑去接住了起司，接著狐狸對烏鴉說：「你是長得不錯啦，但腦子就不怎麼樣了！」

別相信對你說好話的人。

狐狸與樵夫

p. 18–19 幾個獵人正在追捕一隻狐狸，狐狸碰到樵夫，就請樵夫搭救。狐狸說：「好心的樵夫呀，請讓我避一避吧。」樵夫於是要狐狸進到他的屋子裡躲起來。

不久，獵人追了上來。他們問樵夫：「你有沒有看到一隻狐狸？」

樵夫回答：「沒有。」但卻用手指著自己的房子。獵人不解其意，一行人便離開了。

過了一會兒，狐狸從屋裡出來，但未向樵夫道謝。樵夫很生氣，問道：「為什麼你不說謝謝？」

狐狸回答：「我是想道謝的，但我看到你對獵人打暗號，你的言行不一啊。」

言行應該一致——並出於善意。

獅子與老鼠

p. 20–21 一隻獅子正睡得香甜，一隻小老鼠卻在他的臉上踩了過去。獅子被弄醒，大為光火。身材魁梧的獅子抓住小老鼠，準備要殺死他。

老鼠對獅子哭道：「要是饒了我，將來我必對你拔刀相助！」

獅子聽了噗嗤一笑，說：「一隻小老鼠，要幫助像我這樣大的一頭獅子？」獅子發噱，就放老鼠走了。

那天過後沒多久，獅子在森林中行走，不期被補獸網給網住了，獅子非常生氣，怒吼著。

小老鼠一聽到，就立刻跑過來營救他。他看到網子便開始咬。很快地，網子就被咬出了一個大洞，讓獅子得以逃出來！

老鼠說：「你看，你之前還嘲笑我呢。就算是一隻小老鼠，也能救一隻大獅子啊。」

幫助別人永遠不會徒勞無功！

生病的獅子

p. 22–23　有一天，一隻年老的獅子發現自己已經老得無法狩獵了。他想自己已經日薄西山，不覺黯淡神傷地走回家。

就在他緩步回家的路途上，他對一隻鳥説了自己的慘況。很快地，森林裡的動物都知道了獅子的慘事。

其他動物都為獅子感到難過，便一一前去探望他。

獅子又老又虛，但卻精明得很。等隻身孤影的動物走進他家時，都被他輕而易舉地抓來充飢了。很快地，又見老獅子一副快活福態的樣子了。

p. 24–25　一天清晨，來了一隻狐狸。這隻狐狸也很聰明，他慢慢走近獅子的屋子，站在門外，問候獅子是否好了點。

「哈囉，我最要好的朋友。」獅子説：「是你嗎？我看不清楚，你站太遠了。麻煩你走過來一點，説些安慰我的話吧，我老了，就快不行了。」

狐狸趁獅子説話時，仔細打量了一番獅子住家前的地上。

最後，狐狸抬起頭對獅子説：「很抱歉，我得閃了。我現在緊張死了，我看到有很多動物走進你屋裡的腳印，卻沒看到任何一個走出來的腳印！」

從別人身上獲得教訓的人才是智者。

[第二章] 狗和影子

`p. 30–31` 從前有一隻狗，他有一塊上好的肉可以當晚餐。他將肉叼在嘴裡，活像國王一樣得意洋洋地走著。

在他回家的路上，有一條小溪。他路過小溪時，停了下來，望望平靜清澈的溪水。他在水裡看見了什麼？

他看到，有一隻狗正抬頭望著他！那隻狗就與我們快樂的小狗長得一模一樣，甚至嘴裡也叼著一塊肉！

「我要想辦法把那塊肉也給弄到手。」小狗說。

然而，當他張開口想咬住另一塊肉時，他自己口中的肉卻應時從嘴裡掉下來，落到了溪裡頭了！此時他發現，水中那隻狗嘴裡的肉也不見了。

他難過地走回家，那天，他只能在夢裡嚐到吃肉的滋味。

別為了不存在的東西，失去自己原本所擁有的。

給貓掛鈴鐺

`p. 32–33` 一天，所有的老鼠群聚一起，討論貓的問題。「我們一定得想個辦法，躲過貓的追殺，」一隻年長的老鼠說：「他已經吃了我們太多隻老鼠了，我們到底該怎麼辦？」

終於，一隻年輕自信的老鼠站了出來，說道：「兄弟們，相信大家都知道，貓跑得很快，等聽到他的聲音之後再跑，我們就來不及逃了。我們就在他的脖子上綁個鈴鐺吧，那樣聽到叮噹聲時，我們就可以先溜之大吉了。」

「好耶！」所有老鼠齊聲叫好。「我們聰明的年輕朋友可想到了一個妙計了！我們快去買個鈴鐺吧！」

但這就在此時，一隻年長睿智的老鼠開口說道：「等一下，這個計謀確實是很妙，只是，誰要去去把鈴鐺綁在貓的脖子上？」

老鼠們面面相覷，異口同聲道：「對啊，誰要去？」

知易行難。

龜兔賽跑

p. 34–35 一天，兔子嘲笑烏龜動作太慢。烏龜說：「你覺得我速度很慢嗎？不如我們就來比賽賽跑，我一定會贏的。」

「噢，是這樣嗎？」兔子回道：「那我們就走著瞧吧，看誰會贏！」不久，烏龜和兔子同意讓狐狸來擔任這次比賽的裁判。

比賽當天，兔子和烏龜在起跑點上與狐狸會合。他們起跑後沒多久，兔子就把慢吞吞的烏龜遠遠拋在後面了。兔子想她可以停下來好好休息一下，便找了一塊柔軟舒適的草坪休息，旋即沉入夢鄉。

這期間，烏龜持續不斷往前邁進。烏龜雖然跑得很慢，但不敢稍有怠懈。兔子睡了又甜又長的一覺，等她醒來才知事態嚴重！她睡得太久了！她立刻跳起來，全速往前跑，只是為時已晚了，烏龜已經越過終點線了！

緩慢而穩定能贏得比賽。

湖邊的雄鹿

p. 36–37 在一個炎熱的一天，一隻又高又壯的雄鹿停在清澈的湖邊。他低頭喝水，看見自己在水中的倒影。

「我的一雙鹿角實在太帥了！」他說：「那麼強壯又優雅！可是我好傷心我的四條腿這麼瘦，好難看！」

正當此時，叢林裡衝出了一頭獅子，直往雄鹿身上撲過來。雄鹿飛快奔走，他那難看的瘦腿幫他逃得遠遠的，但獅子仍窮追不捨。

很快地，雄鹿就被追趕進了森林，林中樹木茂密，他那對帥氣的鹿角竟被樹枝給勾住了！他奮力掙脫，但鹿角長得太長，掙脫不了。

最後，獅子逮住他，把他給吃了。

人們時常忽略生命中真正重要的事物。

鄉下老鼠與城市老鼠

p. 38–39 有一天，一隻住在城市裡的老鼠去鄉下拜訪朋友。住在鄉下的老鼠見到好友非常高興。

他把最好的晚餐食物拿出來款待訪客，又擔心食物不夠兩人吃，所以自己只吃了一點玉米，而讓好友吃了一些青豆、一塊新鮮起司和一個熟紅蘋果。

城市老鼠吃完了所有東西後，說道：「我的朋友呀，這鄉下怎能住人呢？除了森林、河流、田野和高山，什麼也沒有。每天只能聽鳥叫聲，你一定很膩了吧。」

p. 40–41 「和我一起到城市裡吧！到了那裡，有大洋房可以住，而且每天都有大餐可以吃。只要在城市裡住上一個星期，你就會樂不思蜀的。」於是，兩隻老鼠便出發前往城市。

晚上，他們抵達了城市老鼠的家。城市老鼠對好友說：「我們走了那麼久了，你一定餓了吧！我們趕快來吃晚餐吧。」

他們走進餐廳，城市老鼠找到了一些蛋糕和水果。

「自行享用吧，食物夠我們兩個吃。」城市老鼠說。

「好豐盛的晚餐呀！」鄉下老鼠說：「你真有錢啊，朋友！」就在此刻門被打開，一隻狗衝了進來。兩隻老鼠立刻跳下桌子，跑到地板找洞躲起來。可憐的鄉下小老鼠被嚇壞了！

「別害怕。」他的好友說：「狗鑽不進來的。」

p. 42–43 之後，兩隻老鼠又走進廚房，他們在架子上找到了一個蘋果派。他們享用著蘋果派。

這時，他們卻看到一對晶亮的眼睛正盯著他們瞧。

「有貓！有貓！」城市老鼠叫道，兩隻老鼠迅速鑽進牆壁的洞裡。

等鄉下老鼠喘過氣後，他說：「再見了，我的朋友！你可以在城市與貓狗同住，但我還是喜歡我鄉下的家。

在鄉下，我吃玉米和蘋果時，還會有鳥對我唱歌；住在城市裡，吃著美味的蛋糕和派時，卻會有貓在一旁虎視眈眈。我寧願安心地吃玉米，也不願膽戰心驚地吃蛋糕。」

簡單但安心的一餐，勝過在恐懼中享用大餐。

[第三章] 下金蛋的鵝

p. 46–47 從前有一個人，養了一隻很神奇的鵝，這隻鵝每天都會下一顆金蛋。不久，這人就變得很富有。然而，當他變得越有錢，就愈貪心。

「這隻鵝的身體裡一定是藏了黃金。」他想著：「我要把她肚子剖開，一次把所有黃金都拿到手。」

他便宰殺了鵝，可是卻沒有找到任何黃金。

這人哭道：「一天一顆金蛋，我就該要滿足了。」

貪念會讓人做出蠢事。

熊與旅人

p. 48–49 很久以前，有兩個男人結伴同行，不期遇到了一隻熊。其中一人趕緊爬到樹上，盡量把自己躲在枝葉裡；另一個人則摔倒跌到地上。

當熊走近對他東聞西嗅時，他就屏住呼吸詐死。熊於是很快就走開，因為就像許多人說的那樣，熊是不碰死掉的動物的。

熊走掉了之後，在樹上的男人跳下來，走到朋友的身旁，開玩笑地問道：「剛剛那隻熊在你耳邊說了什麼？」

朋友一臉正經地答道：「他說呀，不要和碰到危險時會丟下你的朋友一起同行。」

真正的好朋友，無論情況好壞都會在你身邊。

牧童與狼

p. 50–51 從前,有一位小牧童在山腳下牧羊,成天一個人看管著羊群,讓他覺得很無聊。

有一天,他想到了一個找樂子的方法。他跑到村子裡,大喊著:「狼來了!狼來了!」

善良的村民聽到就跑出來相助,還有一些人在一旁陪了他一會兒,讓男孩覺得很得意。

幾天過後,他故計重施,又跑到村子裡大喊:「狼來了!狼來了!」村民又跑來幫忙,但半隻狼影也沒見到。

誰知過了沒多久,真的來了一隻狼,開始騷擾羊群。男孩大聲喊叫,叫得比以往還要大聲:「狼來了!狼來了!」

然而,村民之前已上當過兩次,他們以為這次又是男孩在惡作劇,就沒有人出來幫忙,於是整個羊群就被狼給吃光了!

沒有人會相信騙子,即使他說的是真話。

送牛奶的女孩與水桶

p. 52–53 一位農夫的女兒手裡提著一桶牛奶。

她心想著:「我可以把這些牛奶賣了,賺點錢回來,這點錢至少可以買三百個雞蛋,三百個雞蛋又至少可以孵出二百五十隻雞。等小雞長大,我就把牠們拿到市場賣。等賣了小雞,我就有足夠的錢買一件新洋裝。」

「我要穿著美麗的新衣去參加舞會,所有的年輕俊男都會向我求婚,但我會一一拒絕,只想盡情玩樂舞會!」

這妙齡女郎只顧著沉浸在自己的幻想中,沒注意到地上的石頭。突然,她腳踢到石頭,人應聲跌倒,那桶牛奶也被摔到了地上!牛奶就這麼滲透到地下,讓她夢碎!

雞蛋還沒孵出來之前,先別急著數有幾隻雞!

男孩與青蛙

p. 54-55 有一天，一群男孩在一個小湖邊玩耍，有些男孩朝湖裡丟石頭，覺得很好玩。

湖裡住著許多青蛙，一直被男孩們丟的石頭給砸到。

最後，一隻年老富有智慧的青蛙把頭伸出水面，說道：「孩子們，請不要再對我們扔石頭了。」

「我們不過是丟著好玩啦。」男孩們回答。

青蛙說：「我知道啊，只是你們扔的石頭弄傷我們了！你們扔石頭或許只是為了好玩，但是你們的快樂卻造成了我們極大的痛苦！」

一人的快樂可能是他人的痛苦。

守財奴

p. 56-57 有位守財奴把大半的土地賣掉，買了一塊閃閃發亮的黃金。他把黃金埋在一面老舊的牆壁下方，每天都要跑去那裡看看他的黃金。

有一天，他的工人見到他往牆邊走去，便一路尾隨，不久就發現他藏了黃金的秘密。待守財奴離開後，工人就把黃金挖出來偷走。

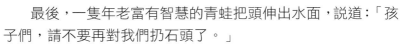

第二天，守財奴發現黃金被偷，又生氣又難過地放聲大哭。

鄰居見狀，知道了詳情，便對他說：「別哭得這麼傷心了，你應該去找塊石頭，把它埋在地下，假裝它是那塊黃金，就跟黃金還埋在那兒時一樣，反正你擁有那塊黃金時，也沒拿它來做什麼呀！」

金錢的真正價值不在於擁有它，而是妥善運用它。

[第四章] 螞蟻與蚱蜢

p. 62–63 一群螞蟻與一隻蚱蜢同住在一片大草原上，螞蟻們總是辛勤工作，希望備妥足夠的食物、有足夠的收穫好過冬。

過得很快活的鄰居蚱蜢，卻不能理解他們的行為，蚱蜢沒多用心去想，只顧著整日唱歌作樂。

初霜降下時，螞蟻才收工，蚱蜢也不再作樂。一個冬日，當螞蟻忙著將穀物搬到陽光下曬乾時，蚱蜢餓得快死掉，便跑去找螞蟻討食物。

「早啊，我慷慨的鄰居。」蚱蜢説：「可以借給我一些糧食嗎？在明年的這個時候之前，我一定會還你們的。」

p. 65 「你自己怎麼沒食物呢？」一隻老螞蟻問他：「一整個夏天草原上滿地都是糧食，那時你在做什麼呀？」

「哦，」蚱蜢一時忘了飢餓，回答道：我每天早晚都在唱歌啊。」

螞蟻説：「既然你可以唱一整個夏天，也該跳一整個冬天的舞吧。」

老螞蟻説完，就回去做自己的工作，唱著螞蟻的歌：「我們螞蟻從不借糧，也從不借給人糧。」

即使在安逸的環境下，也別忘了居安思危。

螞蟻與鴿子

p. 66 有一天，一隻螞蟻走在河邊，對自己說：
「這河水看起來又甜又涼，我一定要喝一點！」

然而就在他正要喝水時，腳一滑，就
跌進了河裡。

「啊！來人啊！拜託，快救救我！
不然我會死的啊！」螞蟻大喊。

一隻停在河邊樹上的鴿子聽到了，便丟了一片樹葉給他，
說道：「爬到樹葉上，你就可以隨樹葉漂到河邊了。」

螞蟻立刻爬到樹葉上，風將樹葉吹到岸邊，螞蟻又回到陸
地上。

「謝謝你呀，善良的鴿子。」螞蟻上岸後對鴿子說：「你
救了我一命，真希望我可以報答你。」

鴿子回答：「再見了，小心別再掉進河裡就是了。」

p. 68-69 幾天後，鴿子忙著築巢，螞蟻見到獵人正舉起槍準備
射她。

螞蟻立刻跑過去，對著獵人的腳狠狠地咬下去。獵人痛得
大叫：「噢！噢！」他手上的槍也掉了下來。鴿子見到一驚，
旋即飛走。

直到獵人離開後，鴿子才又飛回巢穴。她說：「謝謝你，
我的小朋友。你救了我一命。」

小螞蟻開心地跳著，因為他終於能夠幫到好心的鴿子了。

一件善行會帶來另一件善行。

青蛙與公牛

p. 70-71 有一天，一隻公牛走在濕漉漉的田野裡，一隻腳不小心踏到了一群小青蛙，幾乎踩死了全部小青蛙。一隻小青蛙逃過一劫，迅速跳回到媽媽身邊。

「喔，媽媽！」他說：「剛剛我們在玩的時候，有一隻好大的四腳動物踩到我們了。」

「好大？」這隻年長的青蛙問：「有多大？」

青蛙媽媽吸了一口氣，把自己變大後說：「像這麼大嗎？」

小青蛙回答：「哦，比這還要大很多。」

「好吧！那有這麼大嗎？」她又吸了更大一口氣。

「哦，媽媽，比這還要大多了。別再吸氣了，妳會傷到自己的。」

青蛙媽媽不喜歡她的孩子質疑自己的能耐，想把自己變得更大。然而，這一回因為她吸氣吸得太用力，就把自己的身體給脹破了。

過於自信可能會導致自我毀滅。

[第五章] 風與太陽

p. 74-75 很久很久以前，風和太陽在談天，他們無法判斷兩人誰比較厲害。為了找出答案，他們同意進行測試。

他們看到一個旅人經過，就決定試看看誰能先讓旅人把外套脫下。

風開始吹起一陣寒冷的大風，然而風吹得越大，路人就把外套裹得越緊。

接著輪到太陽，他從雲後方露臉，用溫暖柔和的陽光照射著旅人。

旅人感到一陣柔和的陽光暖暖灑在肩上。最後，他坐下來，脫下了外套。顯然地，太陽贏得了這次的比賽。

柔和的力量，比冷酷更加強大。

橡樹與蘆葦

p. 76–77 河邊長了一棵高大的橡樹，它的根牢牢地伸至地下，樹梢高聳天空。橡樹對自己說：「我真是猛呀！沒有什麼能讓我折下腰，我比其他的樹都要來得更高大、更強壯。」

一天，來了一場暴風雨。強風吹打著這棵驕傲的橡樹，橡樹倒進了河裡。河水載著它，往下游流去。途中，它見到了一株長在河邊的細瘦蘆葦。

瘦小的蘆葦直直站著，看著被吹斷的可憐橡樹。橡樹說：「嗨，蘆葦。刮風時，你怎麼沒有被吹斷？你這麼小、這麼弱。」

蘆葦回答：「喔，可憐的橡樹，因為刮風時，我會彎下身子，讓風通過，往它該吹的方向吹去，它不會傷害知道心懷謙卑的生物。」

要想成功，有時就必須低頭。

斧頭與樹木

p. 78–79　很久很久以前，一個男人走進森林，問一棵樹木願不願意給他一些木材，好讓他做斧頭的握柄。樹木覺得這只是一個芝麻小事，所以就給了他一塊上好的硬木。

　　然而，當男人把斧頭上的握柄裝好時，卻立刻開始將森林裡最好的樹木全都砍下來。

　　樹木痛苦地倒在地上，傷心地對彼此說道：「我們因愚蠢而受苦。」

　　只有傻子才會親手把武器交給敵人。

玫瑰與不凋花

p. 80–81　花園裡，一朵玫瑰與一朵不凋花並列開出了花。在一個晴朗的夏日，不凋花對它的鄰居說：「我忌妒你的美麗與甜美的香氣！現在我明白為什麼人人都那麼愛你了。」

　　然而，玫瑰卻悲傷地答道：「唉，我的朋友，我開花的時光很短暫，花瓣旋即枯萎凋謝，那時我也會死去。但你的花永不凋零，即使你被剪下來，也能永生不死。」

　　偉大自會招致問題。

男孩與堅果

`p. 82–83` 有一次，小男孩把手放進一個罐子裡，罐子裡裝滿堅果，他想一手能抓多少就盡量抓住所有堅果。但當他要把手拿出來時，卻發現手太大，沒辦法伸出狹窄的瓶口。

小男孩不想放棄他手裡的堅果，而放聲大哭起來。大人站在旁邊看著小男孩，對他說了一句智慧之言。

「只拿一半，你就能心滿意足的話，那你很輕易就可以拿得到了。」

不要一次嘗試太多。

Answers

P. 26
(A) **①** F **②** T **③** T

(B) **①** branch **②** close **③** happy **④** down

P. 27
(C) **①** and **②** when **③** but

(D) **①** → **④** → **③** → **②**

P. 44
(A) **①** F **②** F **③** F

(B) **①** different **②** quickly **③** wise

P. 45
(C) **①** (a) **②** (a) **③** (c)

(D) **①** while **②** eating **③** fear

P. 58
(A) **①** fine **②** laid **③** greedy **④** killed

(B) **①** T **②** T **③** F **④** F **⑤** T

P. 59
(C) **①** (c) **②** (a)

(D) **①** sold **②** buried **③** went **④** saw

P. 72
(A) **①** F **②** F **③** T

(B) **①** (c) **②** (a)

P. 73
(C) **①** or **②** and **③** When **④** After

(D) **④** → **②** → **③** → **①**

P. 84　　A　❶ powerfully　❷ tighter　❸ took off　❹ won

　　　　　B　❶ F　❷ T　❸ F

P. 98　　A　❶ exploded　❷ farmer　❸ travel　❹ country
　　　　　　❺ bell　❻ mouse　❼ stream

　　　　　B　❶ The ants were harder working than the
　　　　　　　 grasshopper. (T)
　　　　　　❷ The country mouse didn't like living in the city. (T)
　　　　　　❸ Putting a bell on a cat is an easy job for a mouse.
　　　　　　　 (F)
　　　　　　❹ Having gold is more important than using it wisely.
　　　　　　　 (F)

P. 99　　C　❶ What does the story, *The Ants and the Grasshopper*
　　　　　　　 teach us? (a)
　　　　　　❷ What does the story, *The Hare and the Tortoise*
　　　　　　　 teach us? (b)
　　　　　　❸ What does the story, *The Shepherd Boy and the
　　　　　　　 Wolf* teach us? (c)
　　　　　　❹ What is a 'miser'? (c)
　　　　　　❺ What is a 'shepherd'? (b)

Adaptor of *Aesop's Fables*

Scott Fisher

Michigan State University (Asian Studies)
Seoul National University (MA, Korean Studies)
Ewha Womans University, Graduate School of
Translation and Interpretation, English Professor

伊索寓言【二版】
Aesop's Fables

作者 _ 伊索（Aesop）

改寫 _ Scott Fisher

插圖 _ Cristian Bernardini

翻譯 / 編輯 _ 羅竹君

作者 / 故事簡介翻譯 _ 王采翎

校對 _ 賴祖兒

封面設計 _ 林書玉

排版 _ 葳豐／林書玉

播音員 _ Leo D. Schotz / Fiona Steward,

製程管理 _ 洪巧玲

發行人 _ 周均亮

出版者 _ 寂天文化事業股份有限公司

電話 _ +886-2-2365-9739

傳真 _ +886-2-2365-9835

網址 _ www.icosmos.com.tw

讀者服務 _ onlineservice@icosmos.com.tw

出版日期 _ 2020年2月 二版一刷（250201）

郵撥帳號 _ 1998620-0 寂天文化事業股份有限公司

國家圖書館出版品預行編目資料

伊索寓言 / Aesop 原著；Scott Fisher 改寫. --
二版. -- 臺北市：寂天文化, 2020.02
    面；　公分
譯自：Aesop's fables
ISBN 978-986-318-895-7(25K 平裝附光碟片)

805.18   109000891